J·U·P·I·T·E·R

Local Justice in the Chesapeake Country
A 1970s Murder Mystery

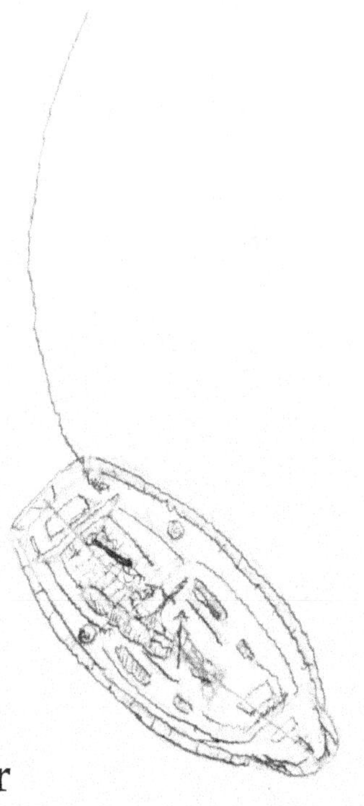

Jim Sayler

Sanidine Books
Rockville, Maryland

Book Cover, "Chesapeake Morning" by James Sayler

Book Design by Robert Henry, righthandpublishing.com

ISBN: 979-8-9858822-0-9

Published by Sanidine Books

You can contact the author at saylerworks@yahoo.com

First Edition, November 2023

TO TERRY ANN

A Great Story in Her Own Right

CONTENTS

CHAPTER 1

Deep Stress

No wonder that robins, hummingbirds, monarch butterflies, and many other of God's gentle creatures, as best they could, were hell bent to leave Chesapeake Bay. Winter lay only a few weeks away. Nature was in deep stress. In the worst way, God's gentle creatures sought the climate mercies of the Deep South.

Blue fish and their prey roiled the water near my boat. Singly and by the squad, blues cut through a school of baitfish, lunging up—some of them out of the water, and then falling back—before swimming off in the further pursuit of killing and eating and storing energy for the great trek to the ocean to the south, their place to spend the winter. As their forefathers had done for thousands of years, the blues had come into the mood. Once again, they had interrupted their cruising, their spying, their monitoring from the depths to strike up at the belly of the nearest school of baitfish, a school that in shallow waters looked like an enormous, hazel carpet come alive. The blues panicked their prey, causing some to leap out of the water moments ahead of being wounded or eaten alive. The rest of the school of baitfish writhed slowly and sought shelter where there was none, slow in reacting to the neighboring cannibals. This multitude of baitfish looked like a slow, wandering, pioneer nation in search of the promised land but under attack on the way from the French, or Indians, or English, Russians, Spanish, or God knows who. The school swam toward the surface, only to turn away and slide into the olive-brown darkness of the depths. As the school of bait fish turned, light from the bright evening sky reflected momentarily off their silver sides, producing a mass of dim flickerings.

Had this performance taken place a few miles to the West on Chesapeake Bay itself, flocks of seagulls and crowds of fishermen in boats, each in their fashion, might have observed and harvested. However, here on the Eastern Shore of the Bay, just off the Wye River, the neighborhood blues swam too far—just a few miles—from the Bay for such an audience. Here the blues held their revels in Dividing Creek of the "Eastern Shore" of Chesapeake Bay. The Creek lay off the Wye River East, just east of the "Middle Bay."

The helter-skelter of baitfish in the murk below me, and the mood produced by that sight, served as an omen that, for the next couple of hours anyway, there would be no merriment and laughter, no song, and no ribaldry aboard my good ship *Jupiter*. Watching the blue fish brought to mind once again incidents of the past few hours that bothered me. The incidents suggested that other dark shapes on the prowl might be monitoring me, might be placing me among the hunted.

The first incident had taken place early Friday night. My friend Edith and I had begun the weekend by supping at the Clam Pier in Galesville, Maryland, a few miles south of Annapolis. The Clam Pier was convenient for starting the weekend because it stood only a half-mile or so from the boatyard that slipped my sailboat, our home for the weekend.

Edith and I had been standing in line at the restaurant, minding our business, when a man next to me became violent for no apparent reason. I'd never seen him before. He shoved me without cause—the line we were in was short. He prepared a repeat. It was crazy. Peter Cave, the owner and manager at the Clam Pier at the time, and a friend of mine, stood nearby. He spotted what was happening and quickly moved Edith and me to a table before I could get into the spirit of the moment and give my new acquaintance some of his own back. Peter afterward commented that the incident was unusual, for the people in Galesville were at peace with one another and happy to help, whatever the circumstances.

The next incident took place after Edith and I had left the Clam Pier. Our departure began our plan to sail the next morning to cross over to the Eastern Shore of the Bay. We carried out our plan to motor a couple of miles to the Rhode River, where we anchored. Our anchorage proved isolated enough for us to have stayed there for a couple of weeks if need be. Twenty-eight feet long, *Jupiter* had room enough for light cruising; she had been designed and built for that, under sail. Drawing only three feet of water, less than some powerboats her size, she would gunkhole into all sorts of shallow coves and rivers. Altogether, she sailed well under her Bermuda rig and over a hull that slipped through the water so efficiently as to show little turbulence, little wake. *Jupiter*, a Morgan 28, lived on as a "daughter" of Charlie Morgan, a yacht designer who had conceived her and whose company in 1968 had built her in Florida.

By habit, I rose a couple of times during the night to check over the boat, to make sure among other things that she remained well anchored. Sometimes a rising wind moved *Jupiter* around the points of the compass, which meant that her anchor might have pulled free, setting her adrift. Other times, the wake of a passing boat rocked *Jupiter* and disturbed me. Now and then I had no good reason for getting out of bed, apart from a set of mind that avoids taking for granted anything on the water.

At midnight, the sound of a motor woke me. Some explorer of the night was passing by, its wake gently rocking *Jupiter*. Getting out of bed and going on deck was the only way to ensure that the skipper of a visiting boat, if preparing to settle for the night, did not anchor too close by and raise the chances of a collision of our boats in a squall, should one appear.

A workboat headed away from *Jupiter* toward the mouth of the Rhode River. There being no work for it in this place, at this hour, the boat seemed out of place for dark wander. Even during normal hours for such a boat—normal meaning just before dawn or during the day—it should have been a mile or so away near the mouth of the West River, working one of the sites where watermen of the Bay lay their lines and traps for catching crabs.

The workboat ran twenty-five feet at most, small as such boats go. A gray-white, flat-bottomed craft probably made of wood, the boat displayed an open hull, its motor located amidships and its small stand-up cabin forward, looking like a small outhouse with a flat roof and windows but without the carved-in crescent moon in its door. The cabins of such boats are too small for luxury or even for challenge recreation, such as night cruising; at best, it provided stand-up shelter from the sun or foul weather. To sleep on any other part of a workboat would be weather chancy, because by design it was, like most other workboats, open, the better to hold the diminished cargoes of Chesapeake fish or bushels of crabs or oysters that it had been designed to hold.

As the workboat was leaving, I remembered having looked around out of habit, when Edith and I were leaving the Clam Pier, to see if we were being followed. Now it was too late and too chilly for considering anything but sleep, so I returned to bed.

~

The third and most ominous incident took place after Edith and I had sailed across the Bay. The incident took place a couple of hours before we had anchored in Dividing Creek. The two of us decided to eat out again rather than go through the trouble of cooking on *Jupiter*. We went to Hattie's Fish Fin, a seafood restaurant in St. Michaels, a few miles south of the Creek where we would spend the night.

We had just been served when the good old boy who had tried to start the fight with me the previous night appeared. Again, he caught me by surprise. He shoved the table where we sat, and caused our chowder and beer to spill, making a mess.

"Do you have to go this far to look for trouble?" I asked, standing up, and getting ready to take him on if need be.

"What are you going to do about it?"

"Advise you to lose 50 pounds and 10 years before you get into your new career."

My friend was big enough, about my size, six foot two, and—in his late twenties—a little younger than I was. His face was red with wind, sun, and drink. His body might have been a showcase for prizes won for excess: too much work, sport, and anger. But he would be bad news in a fight.

"Keep it up, smart mouth," he replied. "You're in for more trouble than you know."

"Take your own advice."

He glared at me for a moment before moving on his way as our waitress came with paper towels and a rag.

"I wonder what's eating him," she said apologetically.

"Does he come here often?" I asked.

"Now and then."

"Probably scares customers away."

She said she was sorry for the mess and left quickly, as if she did not want to discuss the matter. For his part, my new friend took a table on the other side of the room and began to look at the menu. It was only after Edith and I had eaten most of our meal that Hattie's began to get crowded; Edith and I had gotten to the restaurant before the evening trade had begun in earnest. The crowd obscured the view I had of my friend, and in fact, I did not see him again until he made his way to leave the restaurant. At the door, he turned towards me, nodded, and smiled. It was a smile with gaps where he had lost a couple of teeth.

Edith and I returned to *Jupiter*. From a condominium-sized cruiser anchored near *Jupiter* in the St. Michaels harbor came the sounds of a party. Rock music from a distant radio. Laughter. Loud talk. A late-night gathering began to get an early start. Edith and I figured it was time to move on. She grabbed the tiller for progress and good luck. I started the motor, hauled the anchor, and when underway took over the helm from Edith, who gladly gave it up for relaxation in the late afternoon sun, for she had had a rough week.

Enough of the day remained for us to proceed over plate-glass water in comfort over the few miles to Dividing Creek, our anchorage for the night. Our route on the Miles River took us past a land of broad and gentle sights. The land that bordered the mouth of the Wye River proved to be as placid as an English park. Meadows spread out on each side. Reeds crowded the water's edge. Groves of stately trees—many in high color, a few stripped for winter—grew further inland. This was, after all, land that featured estates and preserves of the DuPonts and their kind, a land that also came with retired civil servants, sturdy yeomen and women, watermen, farmers, and the poor tucked in here and there.

Only a couple of boats sat at anchor in Shaw Bay as we passed by. When cruising sailboats and powerboats crowded Shaw Bay at the height of the season (for Shaw Bay was a favorite rendezvous for Chesapeake Bay members of the Cruising Club of America and others), you could be sure that there would be more of a crowd up river. This evening, however, Edith and I had the country to ourselves. Gone were those who a few weeks earlier would have moved at leisure about the mansions and summer places that we passed now and then. Those places now appeared deserted. No one cut the lawn. No one painted a door. I looked aft to see whether any boats were following us or whether there were clouds in the West that should be considered, no promise of bad weather and all that. No problem.

In another half an hour, we reached Dividing Creek. It holds minor fame on the Bay for providing a snug anchorage in winds from all quarters except maybe from the south. I'd been by it several times but had never tried it for the night—now was as good a time as any.

A sign on the bank before us identified the neighborhood as a bird sanctuary. To the left lay a short branch of the creek, for 50 or 60 yards; to the right, the creek proceeded inland some distance, several hundred yards anyway. The chart indicated that the water was plenty deep enough to hold *Jupiter*, and my lead line confirmed it. So, we anchored at the crotch of the long and short legs of the creek, near the foot of a small bluff. At the crest of the bluff, several houses stood, no life apparent in them. In fact, the whole creek was a dead-looking place. It featured no bordering meadows to speak of. Instead, the creek, a tidal estuary, lay long and narrow between two high walls of old trees with foliage so dense as to shade much of the water for most of the day.

Edith and I relaxed in the cockpit: she read a magazine devoted to the good life while I looked for and thought about the blues and the ominous events of the past few hours. Several fish jumped, and others swirled the surface of the waters, another school of blues at work. To ease my mind and to provide fresh meat for breakfast, I broke out a fishing rod and in the fading light began to try my luck.

I heard a motor. *Jupiter* sat 100 yards or so from the river, which lay in clear if distant view. A small workboat appeared, heading upstream just as Edith and I had done before turning into the Creek. It resembled the boat I'd seen the night before. Without changing speed or direction, the boat continued its course up the Wye, past the mouth of the Creek. Only one person was aboard it, so far as I could tell, but I couldn't tell if it was anyone I knew.

I resumed fishing, going through more of my lures without event. I started through them a second time, keeping in mind that only perseverance and results count, the law of competition and success. Creatures of the wild began to stir. A green heron flew by, then a few ducks. Here and there a blue fish stirred the surface of the water again. When Edith and I decided to retire in the cabin for the night, a decision helped by a nip in the air, I had caught no fish.

When it turns chilly with the approach of night, I love to go below because the cabin offers warmth and protection, or at least the illusion of protection. I lit the kerosene lamp, which, with the help of a couple of battery-powered lights, illuminated the main and forward cabins nicely. Soon we listened to quiet music on a portable radio. Edith prepared to read, nesting this way and that on the v-berth in the forward cabin. Outside, not a light could be seen. It was as if Edith and I had suddenly ended up living 300 years earlier, stranded on the frontier of the New World and surrounded by the forest primeval, its noble savages, and other dangers.

When the time came for going to sleep, Edith gave herself to it, but not I, though normally I would have done so in a hunt for warmth and love (specialties of Edith, when she was in the mood) and eventually sleep. This time, however, I sat up for a while.

The sound of a distant motor woke me. When anchoring out, I wake up easily. While I love to be on the water, I don't trust it because of the surprises the water can bring, especially at night.

I put out the lights, pulled back the curtains for a look, and after a few moments, saw the dim shape of a boat emerge from beyond the woods to the left of the mouth of the Creek. The workboat—resembling the one I saw the evening before—carried a green light on her bow and white light astern, heading down the river. She turned into Dividing Creek. Her motor stopped. She coasted. Then her lights went out.

On *Jupiter*, only the anchor light shone, hung outside in the rigging over the bow according to Coast Guard regulations—to inhibit collisions from taking place in the night. *Jupiter* shifted about, so I had to find another view. I opened the louvered screen doors of the main hatch a crack to see if the boat were entering the cove. Again, it was like the one that had gone upstream not long before, though it was hard to see. The night was dark, made darker where we were by the foliage of the cove. The boat coasted toward *Jupiter*, helped by a gentle wind from the south.

No storm forecast and none in sight, I had anchored stern to the wind to reduce *Jupiter*'s pacing at anchor before the wind. *Jupiter* shifted again so that her main hatch and stern faced the workboat. I opened the doors a crack to get a better look. The workboat drew close. I took a winch handle from its pocket next to the main hatch and held it like a club, a few pounds of steel bar with a handle on it. Then I felt around and found a flashlight.

Ghosting along, the workboat touched *Jupiter*, which then listed slightly as someone climbed aboard. I hunched up on the berth next to the main hatch and waited. In a moment, the doors of the hatch opened slowly. The head and shoulders of a large man intruded slowly, coming from lesser darkness to greater darkness. There was just enough light to make out his head and to hit him there with the winch handle. I couldn't get all that much power into the blow, but it was enough to send him sprawling back into the cockpit. After climbing out of the cabin, I shone my flashlight on him.

It was the surly one from the restaurants.

He looked unconscious. I bent down to get his wallet and see who he was. Big mistake. Judging from the blood on his forehead, I had hurt him—but not enough. He stopped playing possum and grabbed me by the arm with a grip that could crack walnuts.

With my free arm, I threw the flashlight at his head. When he flinched, I grabbed the winch handle from my caught arm. He pulled me toward him again. I hit at him in the dark with the winch handle in my free hand and drew a grunt from him.

He got me into a bear hug and began to squeeze the breath from me and break my ribs. I hit him in the side of his rib cage with the handle just as Edith woke up and called out. He loosened his hold. I hit him again and again as he changed his grip and sought my throat, and I hit him once more.

Edith began to scream. Her scream, in addition to the fight he was getting from me, probably unnerved him. He rose and tossed me off in one massive effort, threw a leg over the safety lines on the side of *Jupiter*, and leaped toward his boat, which had drifted a couple of feet away. He barely made it, landing on his chest on the side of his boat, his legs in the water. Stunned for a moment, he scrambled into the cockpit of his boat as I shouted to Edith, "Call the Marine Police again!" As luck would have it, my marine radio was off my boat for repairs. Its antenna only suggested its presence on board, not that my assailant could see it in the dark. Anyway, Edith did not give my bluff away. He started his motor and guided his boat toward the river. I thought about hot pursuit and maybe even running him over and sinking him so he would not forget me, but decided that his was the faster craft, that I did not know the waters well enough to take the chance in the dark, and that I lacked the feel for how the chase would end—was I prepared for his death or mine?

Afterwards, I checked the cockpit and, on the floor, found my flashlight. Next to it lay a long, slender knife, the kind used to fillet fish, a knife which my assailant had left behind. Wondering how I would spend the rest of the night; I went back into the cabin to see how Edith was doing. When she asked in near panic what had happened, I told her the little that I knew, but said I'd hurt the thug and, given his injuries, he probably would not be back. She huddled against the corner of the bunk. After a few minutes, I turned off the anchor light, moved to the cockpit, and sat in the darkness, waiting.

CHAPTER 2

The Search Begins

Edith and I left under power for St. Michaels to file a complaint with the Marine Police about the attack. A downer of a mission on a gorgeous day. No clouds to upstage the sun, a cool tang to the air, and the landscape on a binge of color, it all added up to a great beginning for a sad errand.

It didn't take long to retrace our passage of the previous evening. We arrived at 8:30 and tied up near the Crab Claw at a public dock, in front of a row of houses that belonged to the town's large maritime museum and its acres. A Sunday morning quiet lay upon the town. We were about to search for the police when I noticed a thin, old man puttering around the porch of Hattie's, which was near our dock. I asked if he worked for the restaurant, and he said yes.

"I saw the two of you last night and the man who caused the trouble. I had to clean up the mess after the dust-up," he continued.

"Do you know the name of the waitress and is she local?" I asked.

He paused before saying, "Suzie, I think. I saw what happened at your table. That was Earl Johnston who did that. Suzanne Miller's the name of the waitress. She lives in town with her parents."

"Where does Earl Johnston live?" I asked.

"He's a local boy. His family came up from the Carolinas a few years ago, so he's not all that local. The family lives down near Knapp's Narrows, I believe. Earl does odd jobs down there. Works the water some. Uh… watch out, Earl's mean."

"What family does he have?"

"Don't know exactly. Earl's wife was killed a couple of years ago. Since then, he moved back in with his parents. They're redneck rich. That means they have only a little more money than most. You think Earl attacked you last night?"

"He left this knife."

"He's trouble, all right. Crazy trouble. Not like most of the people here. You'd better report it to the police. They should be around here shortly in their boat"

"That's why I'm here."

"You could also report it to the town or state police"

"Thanks. I'll wait for the cops on the water. I've dealt with them before."

Why not wait? My new acquaintance, Earl Johnston, was no-where to be seen. I didn't know for sure but thought the Marine Police would probably be the ones most responsible for investi-gating what happened at the site of the crime, water being their beat. In fact, it wasn't long before a sturdy, medium-length, outboard motorboat entered the St. Michaels harbor, a boat open to the sky, except for its light gray canvas top. It flew the state flag of Maryland.

Edith and I motored over to the police boat, in which two Marine Police sat, dressed in neat, gray uniforms. Each was beefy, clean-shaven, and reserved. One was young; the other pushed middle age. After I finished my account, the older one said he would file the report and see what could be done. The younger policeman said he remembered the name Johnston from a big trial a couple of years before, a murder trial. Some other man had been convicted of killing a Johnston woman, probably the wife of the man in question. The older cop con-firmed what the old man had said about Johnston's bad name. The cop went on to say that Johnston was supposed to have re-formed after he'd gotten married. But, after Johnston's wife died, he had gone crazy and had been put away for a few months in an asylum. The policeman said that he did not realize that Johnston had been released from the asylum under a doc-tor's care—couldn't have been out for long.

While we talked, the young cop kept looking at the knife I had given him when first reporting the incident. I had picked up the knife with a cotton towel after the attack, thinking that it might have fingerprints that could prove useful.

"You can be contacted at the address you gave us, the apartment?" he asked.

"Yes. Tonight. You'll have to call Annapolis… Pasadena, actually."

"I know it," the cop said.

"That's where I live. I rent an apartment there. I'll sail back today."

"Will that be safe?" Edith asked.

"Probably. The punk who attacked me needs the dark to be brave," I said from tentative wisdom.

"He gave you a hard time at the restaurants, Robert," Edith reminded me with a wifely attention to truth.

"Well… anyway, he thinks I've got a UHF radio on board. He thinks I could call for help."

"He didn't think so last night," Edith continued.

"We don't know what he thought. Anyway, who knows what he was thinking," I replied. "If he got chased off in the dark, why would he return during the day?"

"Whatever you say, Mr. Chappell," the older officer said. "Where do you keep your boat?"

"Rudd Yard. On the West River. Near Galesville. Slip 105."

I had to take the cop's warning seriously. My first step was to protect Edith. She objected to my sailing back alone, but I persuaded her that, if any trouble developed, her ignorance about how to handle herself on the water would hurt both our chances, not help them. So, Edith phoned a friend of hers.

Someone with the improbable name of Lady Kilmur, or Melissa Kilmur, whom she had told about our plans for the weekend. Kilmur on the spot arranged to have her maid drive to St. Michaels and pick up Edith at the marine museum. I wasn't keen about sailing back myself, considering the hazard. I was even less inclined to leave *Jupiter* away from home port and, considering that Earl Johnston might be up for more play, open to vandals.

The engine on, I maneuvered *Jupiter* past the Maritime Museum's Bay lighthouse—squat, old but still white, wooden—that overlooked the harbor. No longer did the lighthouse guide the wandering sailor. It merely diverted the tourist and heightened the public's idea of the wonders of the sea. All went well from the St. Michaels harbor to the Miles River. With plenty of room available, I put up the sails, after which I returned to the cockpit and turned *Jupiter* north, to go before the wind.

I made the Western Shore and the mouth of the West River by dusk with no workboat in sight. As night grew out of dusk, I guided *Jupiter*, sails furled and motor on, under her namesake in the heavens to Galesville and the Rudd Yard. I cut the motor near the docks and ghosted into my slip by the half-light from the dock lamps and by the lesser light from the moon. No wind. I secured *Jupiter* and got off her, ready to head toward car and home. A man dressed in a business suit approached me in the dock, illuminated by a few dock lights. His suit and dark skin blended into the night, making him hard to see at first.

"You Mr. Chappell?" he asked.

"Yes."

"There's a problem with Mr. Johnston. He's the man you filed a complaint about this morning at St. Michaels. I'm Saugers. I'm a detective with the Maryland State Police. I'd like to talk to you about him."

"Good! I'd like to do the same about him. He hasn't had the crust to file a complaint about me, has he?"

"Not hardly. Can you account for your time today, Mr. Chappell?"

"Nothing but sailing. That's what I did after filing my complaint this morning. It was a long trip in light wind. I just got in, as you can see."

"When did you depart from St. Michaels?"

"Eleven o'clock, this morning. What is Johnston's problem?"

"He's been found dead. Please come with me. I'd like you to look at some photographs and ask you a few more questions."

CHAPTER 3

Puzzle

Sunday evening began with a question: what's the score? The question came to me when I opened the door to my apartment. Earl Johnston's death and the way it had up-ended my life stopped at my apartment. It lay in order. Whatever or whomever was on the prowl had not made it to my place.

The memory of how the state troopers had taken me to a barracks near Annapolis for questioning lingered. The cops did not waste time. For them, I reviewed Johnston's attack on me and how I had slept in *Jupiter*'s cockpit in case he returned. When they asked for proof that I had spent the night as adver-tised, I reminded them of Edith, my on-the-scene witness. Had I ever met the dead man before his attack? Yes, and I reviewed our encounters.

They asked if I had used the knife.

No, it wasn't mine. I'd found it after Johnston had left. Hadn't they dusted it for fingerprints, I asked?

No answer.

Their questions suggested that more than blows had killed Johnston. My guess was born out when the detectives showed me photographs of my assailant's corpse. At first, I didn't recognize Johnston. The angle of the photos distorted his features. He looked as if, at the moment of death, he had been in the midst of a strange aerobic dance step. Earl Johnston had been a powerful fellow brought low by someone who had brought more force to bear than he could draw on. Maybe more than one assailant had attacked him.

I had taken a close look at his face in the photos. A large bruise—a blue, bloody lump as large as a silver dollar—appeared on his forehead, probably where I had hit him with the winch handle. Thirty cuts or more disfigured his face, thin cuts, not slashes. Earl had held still for a whole lot of grief, if he had been conscious at the time of his surgery. In fact, the cuts extended to most of his body. It was a torture killing. The police assumed, or so one of the detectives said, that the cuts most likely had bled Johnston to death, though the police lab and the medical examiner's office continued to check on the cause of death.

The police were volunteering more information to me than they would have done normally. Why they would make the effort was beyond me. The reservations that the police often have about journalists and their professional prying did not help, especially since the newspaper I worked for, the *Anne Arundel Herald*, lacked status, for it lived in the small of it all each evening except Sunday. It existed as just a small daily. It lacked status because it stood second in circulation to the *Capital*, the other daily in Annapolis, and the *Herald* was only three years old compared to the start the *Capital* got in 1887. I too stood at a disadvantage with the police, being new to working with them as a journalist in Annapolis. However, I had sailed for years in waters local to Annapolis; during my land time, I had gained at least a working knowledge of the city.

Until coming to Annapolis, I had worked as a general assignment reporter for a couple of daily newspapers in New Jersey, in suburbs that viewed the New York City skyline across Hudson River. I had quit the last job as the paper was laying me off as an economy move. Chesapeake Bay had served as a classroom for me during the summers when I was growing up, weekend sailing jaunts in my maturity, and as a source of the better life now that I was mature. After getting a divorce, I moved to Annapolis. Annapolis offered easy access to rural Maryland on its Western and Eastern Shores.

I met Edith at a seafood festival in Annapolis. We started seeing each other whenever I got down from New Jersey a few months before coming to work for the *Herald*. With Edith, my itch for getting settled grew strong; living alone without family nearby was no way to get old. So, a move to Annapolis, the State Capital of Maryland, looked like the right move. My career would be served by a fresh start in a place I knew something about, particularly since Annapolis often offered many events that could be converted to news. Centered in the Maryland legislature, Maryland politics plus the mix of local socializing livened my work with the varied reporting it offered. As an almost suburb of Washington, D.C., and Baltimore, Maryland, Annapolis offered a faint promise of maybe, someday, hiring on as a reporter for a major publication such as the *Washington Post*. Yes, a pipe dream. Quite persuasive too was the gift Annapolis (which prided itself as "the sailing capital of America") offered of quick access to Chesapeake Bay, and the restorative powers and poetry offered by the water.

As a journalist, I had yet to meet many Maryland troopers or local cops. Knowing cops on rare occasions can pay off as a journalist, particularly when they come to know and trust you. Many police are put on their guard by reporters; they do not trust them, because of the nosiness of reporters and the press's making information public that, in the opinion of many cops, should remain private to reduce the complications that arise in solving crimes and administering law and order. Police secrecy reduces clutter that comes from premature publicity that can impede investigations and the road to justice, especially when it comes to murder. My theory held that the less the police said and the more I said to fill the silence worked to their advantage because of information that I might inadvertently release. Maybe the cops sought a lead through emotions I might show.

Sometimes, however, second sight came to some officers, who, influenced by curiosity and a broad perspective, were less given to secrecy. Those cops, especially detectives in search of information or clues about a case such as murder or assault, would in private sometimes volunteer information to a reporter in the name of sharing information to gain some. In general, however, my perspective about police required keeping in mind that they lived as a brotherhood bound by fears of surprise violence from whatever quarter. This brotherhood distanced, even isolated, often as a state of mind many, if not most, officers from reporters and the public. The hazards and stresses of enforcing the daily rules required longevity of patience, which only compounded why their work was so difficult.

I phoned my lawyer, an old family friend who had moved to Annapolis; and, at that late hour, waited for him to come to the police barracks. He was cautious at first. After the police admitted they would not charge me with anything, even though technically I was a suspect, my lawyer said it was all right for me to tell them what I knew. As it turned out, the cops put me on a kind of parole, in that they urged me to keep in touch with them and tell them if I planned to leave the area.

What could I do? Barricade my apartment and take monastic vows? I still had no idea why a stranger would go out of his way to assault me. Now, that stranger was dead. Was anyone else after me? The chance of an unseen connection between me and more violence was possible, maybe probable; and yet there appeared to be no way of anticipating more violence, short of checking out the remains of the dead man's career, digging up the bones of his life. Why take the chance that my assailant had been just the unpleasant face of bad luck, and the assault just a number picked at random?

I had to start looking without delay, while news of the dead man's fate remained fresh enough to prompt talk about what he had been like. Gossip, to the extent it was available and depending on its quality, could give me a good idea of why Earl had acted as he had—gossip, a benediction the living often bestows on the dead, unable to reply in kind.

One possibility was to return to Earl Johnston's haunts on the Eastern Shore. Going by boat tempted me. That way I might avoid arousing suspicions, or so I rationalized the option. I would be an outsider from the city; for I was a man marked by city clothes and city habits. My best hope would be reality, to be what I what presented myself as, just an ordinary reporter writing a feature story in his spare time about a bizarre murder and a slice of life from Maryland's Eastern Shore. The truth of the matter was that I wanted to travel by boat, my boat, because when under stress I gained comfort and security in it. The boat meant living cheaply, like working out of my apartment. Being out of nautical fashion enough to discourage a second glance by most people, *Jupiter* should provide camouflage and enable me to fit into my surroundings, for she excited little envy.

As for choosing a car over a boat, the superior speed of a car, at least my car, offered a limited advantage. It was easier to drive down the wrong road in a car than using a boat to follow a creek because speed robbed judgment. My old Cadillac, or even a rented car—given its unknown frailties and potential for breaking down, not to mention the discomfort of sleeping in it—would be no more able to escape from another car than *Jupiter* could escape a motorboat if I fell into trouble. Moreover, I could always find some way of renting or borrowing a car over there. At least, that was my justification for the moment. A triumph of confidence over experience.

I phoned the *Anne Arundel Herald* and got Marley DeVon, my boss. As a staff of a tight-budget newspaper publisher, I had to work hard for her to grant me a week's vacation, even after telling her about the attack, what had happened to me, and mentioning I might find news in my hunt. Before calling her, I thought about quitting my job. Moving on, being a nomad, was one way to cope with the threat of another attack. Travel to another part of the country represented another defense alternative. I could hope for anonymity, for I had no wife or family to tie me down, just a girlfriend for whom I really cared. I had money in the bank from an inheritance that had also included my old Cadillac, a symbol of better times and the perishability of status technology. Realistically, however, that extra wad would be only enough to subsidize my comforts and too small to live on for long. Further, I liked my job and the people around me at work, and I was getting tired of being a nomad, tired of quitting a job when I got restless. I could move without ever realizing why my life had been in danger and might continue to be so.

It was the middle of Monday morning when I got out of my car and walked down to *Jupiter*. Someone had bashed in an extension of her bow pulpit on the starboard side. The once gracefully rounded "fence" of chromed tubes of steel looked as if someone had assaulted it with a sledgehammer, beating the crap out of the pulpit. I loaded *Jupiter* with enough gear and supplies for a week or more of cruising (supplementing the several days of supplies normally carried on board), then walked to the yard office to report the damage. As I entered, Tom Pemberton, the yard manager, was on his way out.

"Somebody's staved in the bow pulpit on my boat. How come nobody heard it and stopped it?" I asked.

"Don't know. Nobody here, I guess. The boys in the yard saw it this morning. Probably done sometime last night. We don't have enough trouble here to keep a guard. I was going to call you."

"Can't it be bent back into shape?"

"Maybe. But you'd be able to see the damage. It would look rough. Uh, you want us to replace it?"

"When can you get to it?"

"Sometime next week, Mr. Chappell."

"The damage was done in the yard while *Jupiter* was in her slip. Looks like someone just hit her with something heavy."

"Come to think of it, maybe we should post a guard. We had minor, teenage problems last year with vandals, but nothing this year, so far. At least until your boat. Better contact your insurance company, Mr. Chappell. It'll cost you or them $300 to replace it, perhaps less. I'm sorry it happened, but we're not liable. I sure hope we don't have to hire a guard again like we did last year. That would mean higher dock fees. 'Course, we didn't need the guard after the doctor's son was caught. I told you about that, didn't I?"

"Yes. Is he out of jail?"

"I think so. Hasn't been back here, though. I'll get the boys started on your bow pulpit if you like." Pemberton, a retired, six-foot-tall, fit, ex-Marine officer who believed and practiced a life of coming to the point, looked at me intently.

"I'm going on a short cruise, Mr. Pemberton. Maybe you could do it when I get back."

"Just say the word. A sound bow pulpit adds to the safety of running a boat."

"Right. Why do you think the pulpit was bent in?"

"Probably somebody's idea of fun, Mr. Chappell. Or, maybe somebody doesn't like you. I'm sorry about it. Your insurance company should be able to help you. Wish the yard could assume responsibility for it."

The yard could do so, I thought, since the yard bore responsibility for the safety of the boats it berthed. Since the Rudd Yard chose not to, I could take the case to a local court. The best that I could expect there would be local justice and, if that did not suit me, there would be more legal hassle, not worth the time or money. Moreover, I would probably be invited to look for another yard for my boat. That meant time wasted for such a search, and more frustration for me because of the shortage of boat slips on the Bay.

~

I turned to go when Pemberton said, "Mr. Chappell, you know that the police have been around, asking questions."

"I imagine so."

"There's talk that you were tied in some way to the killing of that fellow on Tilghman Island, Earl Johnston."

"He boarded my boat in the middle of the night and attacked me. I hit him with a winch handle until he took off. You don't see me in jail, do you?" I asked with a smile.

"No." Pemberton smiled.

"Are you sure Earl was murdered?" I asked, curious to see what the police might have revealed. "I didn't know him."

"You didn't know him!?"

"Nope. A stranger."

"It's in this morning's paper. He was cut up bad. You didn't know him?" Pemberton said.

"He tried to start a couple fights with me—in the Clam Pier on Friday night. Hattie's Clam House, in St. Michaels, on Saturday night. I'd never met him before that."

"That's strange."

"Sure is."

"Here's the morning *Baltimore Sun,* in case you haven't read it," Pemberton said, picking it up off his desk and handing it to me.

I'd been so concerned with the police and sorting out what had happened, I'd forgotten to buy a paper. Unprofessional of me. A glance or two through it revealed on page three that someone had found Earl Johnston late Sunday morning, by Knapp's Narrows, a couple of miles from his parents' house. Earl had died two or three hours after midnight. Police said they were looking for a suspect or suspects. Pemberton told me to keep the paper.

"The cops talked to me about the murder," I said.

"They were looking for you on Sunday afternoon. Called me up at my place, and I explained that I did not know any-thing about the death," Pemberton replied.

"They found me Sunday evening as I came into my slip."

"The police were also talking to Earl's brother, Nestor."

"Really?" I asked.

"His brother, Nestor, works in the yard here. He's been here for a couple years. The police took him in for questioning this morning."

"He's a suspect?"

"Don't know for sure," Pemberton replied.

"Could Nestor have damaged my boat for revenge?"

"Couldn't say, Mr. Chappell. Nestor's not vengeful like his brother was. Maybe a little sly, sometimes. I don't think the two brothers got along well. You know, I hate to keep on saying this, but your best bet for financing your boat repairs, Mr. Chappell, is your insurance company. You are insured?"

"Yes, the boat's insured, and I can pay. I remember your misgivings about the reluctance of writers when it comes to paying. So, you knew Earl?" I asked Pemberton.

"By sight only," Pemberton responded with a smile.

"Was Earl over here Friday night, at the yard?"

"Yes," Pemberton said. "He'd won big money, or so he said. Nestor came in for his paycheck, and Earl came in with him, bragging about the money. That's what I told the police. Earl said he planned to celebrate, starting with a fine supper at the Clam Pier. Wasn't going to treat his brother, though. I think he wanted to rub in his good luck. Every now and then Earl would drop by to borrow money from Nestor."

"When do you think the cops will let Nestor go?" I asked.

"They may not. Who knows?"

Detective John Byrne called my cruise a poor idea. It could keep me from coming in on short notice for more questioning. He drawled that it was odd that, having reported an assault with deadly intent, I would not stick around to see how the police investigation of it would go, or that I valued my life so little that I would go adventuring and risk it again. Further, only a fool would conduct his own police investigation. And, I couldn't count on close police protection if I got into trouble in Earl John-ston's country, he concluded. I read Detective Byrne in part as using his expressed doubts as a test to draw out of me how much truth there was in my account. I read Byrne as experienced in police work but not bored by the tedium of one detail after another. All this fitted into a body shorter than I was, and with an acceptable balance between comfort around his waist and energy.

Only when I asked Byrne what he had on his mind—that is, did he have any more questions, as long as I was there? And only after I promised to keep in touch with him, did he relent. He couldn't have had any evidence linking me to the death of Johnston. At best, I was a relevant witness to how Johnston spent a couple of the final hours of his life. So, why was Byrne so uptight about my remaining available? Probably because he was uptight in general. He didn't like loose ends, and in his view, my independence made me just that.

After leaving Byrne's office, my chief concern became crossing the Bay by *Jupiter* and reaching Knapp's Narrows on Tilghman Island before night. With one thing stumbling over another in my preparations for leaving, I did not get underway until shortly before noon. To make up for lost time, I motored down river to the Bay instead of waiting for the wind to blow *Jupiter* there. Had little choice. The water would not help me. As rivers go, the one I was on, the West River, belongs to the broad and usually somnolent bodies along the coast rather than the narrow, often faster, fellows inland by the mountains. Motoring was also called for because the only other potential help from nature, the tide, counted at that hour for the precious little current that there was.

It took almost an hour on the West River to reach the Bay, where I hoisted sail. After that, plenty of time and opportunity remained to back away from the tight concerns of land, to forget for a moment about murder and assault, and to concentrate instead on getting to my destination. Forgetting meant putting my hands into a kind of Fate named *Jupiter*. I could think of *Jupiter* as a support, a fiberglass friend valued in part for the sake of convenience and the strong hope for something better, instead of thinking of her as a cold, distant planet, a pinprick of light in the night sky. *Jupiter* supported me in the immediate and crimped business of reaching the Narrows without running into Poplar Island, crimped because the wind was blowing from the south and the lower Bay, slowing my progress into the very direction in which I wanted to go. I turned *Jupiter* toward the Eastern Shore, and on a starboard tack started down the Bay.

The eye and the mind had a few items to consider. Turning aft, as I had seen many times before, I saw the mouths of the West and South Rivers become so indistinct in the distance that it took a second look to tell exactly where they were. They lay several miles away to the Northwest, light hazy sections in the long gray-green and gray-auburn line that made up the Western Shore. *Jupiter* sailed in the "Middle Bay," whose waters now lay flat, defined by land only slightly less flat. A cluster of radio towers further to the north in Annapolis and the even more distant traceries of the Chesapeake Bay Bridges, still further north, offered most of the relief to an otherwise monotonous skyline.

These bland scenes belied certain deceptions in these waters, an argument for vigilance on the Bay even when relaxed. Names offered a light example: the South River lay north of the West River. However, Knapp's Narrows, my destination, offered a more serious deception. If all went well, my passage would put me there before dusk. Getting there late could put me at risk, given the peculiar pattern for the navigational aids there. Normally, when you take a boat into a harbor most places on the East Coast of the United States, you follow a system of buoys and other navigational markers for guidance, to keep from exiting the channel you were in and running aground in the bordering shoals. The system is easy to remember: "Red right return." Keep the red buoys to the right when you return to port or go up river, and your boat will normally be in the channel. What made Knapp's Narrows tricky was having to remember to reverse the pattern. In this instance, opposites applied to the buoys and telephone poles stuck in the water. Red left, into the channel that leads to the Tilghman Island canal. Only when turning around and heading back to the Bay would you keep Black navigational aids to starboard, or the right of your vessel. Why the Powers That Be reversed the pattern, I don't know.

As the afternoon drew on, the wind rose slightly and changed direction, blowing gently head on from the south. I started *Jupiter*'s engine and began to motor toward Knapp's Narrows.

In principle, sailing should be all quiet and ease as the wind whispers the boat along. The wind whispered all right, but still from the wrong direction. At the rate with *Jupiter* under sail, it could be midnight before she would make the Narrows. Pure sailing under those circumstances could prove to be expensive and even dangerous—namely giving the Bay in undecided weather a chance through a quick and nasty squall at pounding my boat with no escape for me. Trying to negotiate the entrance to the Narrows in the dark in foul weather was no sport for anyone such as myself, who was weak in these parts on local knowledge. The shoals at that entrance were legend. No rocks lay there, rocks to gut the belly of a hull; just mud and sand that could suck onto *Jupiter*'s keel and hold the whole boat fast until the wind rose in darkness and pushed her further toward the shore, toward even shallower waters. In those waters, as a mortar and pestle pounds and grinds herbs and spices, the growing waves would pound *Jupiter* on the floor of the Bay.

Wouldn't you know, the wind died, offering *Jupiter* little hindrance to progress. So little wind remained that, even under slow engine power, I was able to pick up the newspaper that Pemberton had given me. This time I read its account of the murder The main news: the mutilated body of Earl Johnston had been found late Sunday morning propped up against the back wall of a gas station next to Knapp's Narrows, a couple of miles from where Earl's parents lived. So, Edith and I had reported the assault on us at about the time Earl's body had been found, or twelve hours or so after he had boarded *Jupiter*. The only additional news to me was that three persons survived the victim. The father, Albert T. ("Carney") Johnston. The mother, Mauvene, but known as Mae. And Earl's brother, Nestor.

∼

The day drew on, approaching dusk. It was getting late. The tack I had sailed before turning the motor on had taken *Jupiter* close to the Eastern Shore. This new position gave me the chance to cut the time and distance to Knapp's Narrows by taking a short cut through Poplar Narrows, named after the small island that lay just off the Eastern Shore of the Bay.

"Broads" would have been a better name for the place than "Narrows," because the water between the shore and the island lay wide, flat, and shallow. Only a couple buoys and day standards populated the Narrows, which ran several miles long and whose markings often lay beyond sight. So, the compass and chart set the course for the boat. My depth finder served as a backup. The depth finder consisted of a lead line—a length of line, flagged in intervals of a yard, and attached to a ringed hunk of lead. Thrown overboard and hauled up out of the water, it offered a cheap, antique, effective way of seeing how much water *Jupiter* carried under her, often no more than a foot, for a boat that carried a three-foot draft. I had never gone all the way through Poplar Narrows before, so finding and keeping within the Poplar Island channel required stowing the newspaper and paying full-time attention to my course.

During my passage, I remembered a kindness shown me a couple years earlier on Tilghman Island near Poplar Island. I had been sailing on another, smaller boat, one with an outboard motor. Almost no wind. I had been motoring for a couple hours and began to worry about running out of gasoline. I pulled into a creek and up to a dock where several Eastern Shore men stood, dressed for fishing.

I asked if they knew of a gasoline station nearby where I could fill up *Jupiter's* fuel tank. One of the men said that the station was too far.

"I've got extra gas," he said.

"How much do I owe you?" I asked.

"Nothing. Take it. It's a gift."

I filled the tank, offered him money again, and again he said no. It was a gift.

Jupiter made Knapp's Narrows late in the afternoon. Enough time remained for me to stand off the entrance and watch how a couple of workboats and cabin cruisers negotiated their way, and to see if the channel had shifted enough to make the charts wrong. If light and weather were right, you could make your way through the entrance of the Narrows by the look of the water. Small light green or buff waves, or breaking waves, indicated suspect shoals, too close to the surface of the Bay for comfort. Dark greens and blues suggested the channel. Not so this time, however. The Bay water mirrored a sky gone gray. Nevertheless, *Jupiter* made her way without event, making the appropriate turns, keeping to the proper side of the navigational standards. It pays to obey the laws of man and Nature.

Soon *Jupiter* had reached the Narrows proper, which, as a canal without locks, cuts across Tilghman Neck. Here the Narrows was no more than 30 or 40 yards wide. After a few moments, the drawbridge came into view.

I tied *Jupiter* to a dock next to the restaurant I was after, on the Bay-side of the bridge. Dawn would put my boat near its shadow. Old-fashioned, steel-skeleton walls, painted black, comprised the structure of the bridge. It connected Tilghman Island with Tilghman Neck and the roads that led miles and miles away to urban America. The bridge had its keeper, housed in a small shack built near the middle of the bridge. The keeper would raise the bridge for boats with height, usually sailboats, using the Narrows as a shortcut to the Choptank River and to Oxford and Cambridge, Maryland. Those two towns on the Eastern Shore served as yachting centers.

Just before tying *Jupiter* fast to a dock, I thought for a moment about the late Earl Johnston. This had been his country. Where had he lived? Why did he die as he had? Why had he sought me out and attacked me?

CHAPTER 4

The Half Way House

Judging from what it looked like on the outside, the Half Way House Restaurant would be hard to remember. What passed for style was ordinary—run-down here, spruced-up there. It looked as if the builder began by constructing a one-story country bar on the slope by the side of the road next to the drawbridge. His ambition swelled as he continued. By the time he finished, he had two stories by the pier. You walked into the main floor of the restaurant directly from the road. Primed by the look of the exterior, you would expect to see a dark, bare, scarred, wooden floor supporting a few wooden chairs and tables to the side of a dance floor, a jukebox in the corner, maybe a two-man band stand, and, before you, a bar.

Wrong.

The main room contained fifteen or so tables, each draped with a white tablecloth, each table having a full complement of four metal and plastic-covered chairs, like those for a family breakfast nook. Basic furniture. No darkness in the place. All this helped give the restaurant the look of an honest, gentile place, where country people in their Sunday best like to go to for a polite weekend afternoon or evening meal.

The restaurant also attracted the folks from the Bay, especially those traveling in long, new, expensive sailboats and power-boats. These were people who seldom felt the need to belong to the jet set, because they had their own monied way of life going for them, with enough style to sugar anybody's donut.

Once you took a second look at it, the restaurant offered a couple main attractions. Its name was one. Instead of being a refuge for folks trying to trade a life of crime for one of virtue, the name, Half Way House, came from its site, half way between Chesapeake Bay and Harris Creek. Another attraction was the restaurant's tasty food. On the few times when I had stopped by for a meal, the restaurant had served fresh clams and oysters, harvested in local waters by local people. On the way to the men's room, you might see a couple of cooks sitting at a table, levering open clams and oysters with oyster knives. The seafood was fresh, a condition often harder to find than true love. And, the price was right.

When I walked in just as supper was due, only a couple of the restaurant's tables were occupied. The hostess came toward me, beaming with chaste friendship and hope, and led me to a table next to a fogged-up window that overlooked the canal. "Betsy will be your waitress."

"What's tasty and cheap?" I asked Betsy, who took over

from the hostess.

"Everything on the menu," she said as she handed it to me. The broiled blue fish appealed to me, so I ordered it. When she returned with it a few minutes later, I asked her whether the police had found out anything about the death of Earl Johnston.

"Not that I know of," Betsy replied guardedly.

"I haven't gotten to the police yet," I explained. "I'm a reporter from Annapolis."

"Really?" She smiled broadly. Tall, built with angles that were turning into curves, she must have still been in high school.

"Yes. I'm writing a feature story about the murder. I'm going to spend a couple days writing a background piece."

"What's a background piece?"

"It's an article that describes the background to some news event. Right now, I want to tell what the people and the country on Tilghman Island are like, so the murder will have a home to the big city folks." Normally I would not explain much about news or a feature I was working on. But, Betsy was cute and had curiosity.

"Have a home?"

"So, people will see what the roots of the murder were. That's my hope, anyway."

"You're not going to make fun of the people around here, are you?" Betsy asked.

"No. I just want to make the murder understandable to the people in the city. This is conservative country—nothing changes its ways around here much, whether people want change or not.

Given a choice and opportunity, people here are kind. When someone is sliced up, murdered, as Earl Johnston was, it still counts for something here. In the city, people are murdered every day, and you might never read about it in the newspapers, unless there was something exceptional about it. It's too common an event there to be much news. Here, murder is exotic. It is a radical event, and any radical event is news."

"You sure throw the bull, mister. But you've got a nice smile." She smiled again and paused to check its effect on me before leaving for a couple minutes. Business being slow and my being a distraction, she returned and asked, "Are you really a reporter?"

"Don't you believe me?"

"Next you're going to tell me that you work for the *Washington Post* or the *Baltimore Sun*."

"I work for the *Anne Arundel Herald*, normally, but this is freelance, maybe for the *Post*."

"Before I graduated from high school last year, I worked on the school paper. I'd need college to be a reporter, I guess."

"Not necessarily. You might find something on a small newspaper. You might try one them over here. Do you know the Johnstons?"

"No, not really."

"Do you know where they live?"

"A mile or two on the road towards St. Michaels, I think. They used to eat here, you know."

"No, I didn't."

"They got thrown out of here about a month ago. They drank too much and started arguing. Mrs. Hughes, the hostess, called the police after the old man stabbed one of our cats with a fork."

"That's funny."

"No, it wasn't. I saw it!"

There was an awkward pause before I said, "I mean, it was strange."

She turned and left. When she returned with the next helping of food, I apologized, saying that I had laughed because I thought she was pulling my leg.

"Are you sure you weren't laughing at the trouble that poor cat was in?"

"Yes, I wasn't. What was the reaction around here when people found out about the killing... the Johnston killing?" I asked.

"Well, you know they found the body just across the Narrows. You can see that gas station out the window. Mostly people were talking about the peculiar ways that the Johnstons have. They're not from around here, you know."

"Are you sure?" I asked.

She replied, "They've lived here for ten years or so. Came up from the Carolinas, I believe. Actually, you really should talk to Mrs. Hughes, the hostess—she knows more about them than I do."

Mrs. Hughes, a couple tables away, heard her name mentioned, looked over, smiled, and came by.

"Is your meal satisfactory, sir?" she asked, with a glance at the waitress.

"Yes, Ma'am. Fine service too."

"He's a reporter from the *Washington Post*," the waitress said. "He's writing a story about the murder and about the people around here, how they're reacting."

"Do you know Peter Harwood?" the hostess asked.

"Not personally. I just write an occasional feature for the *Post*. I'm a reporter for the *Anne Arundel Herald*."

"Peter is an editor with the *Post*. He works, I believe, as an editor on stories about Maryland and Virginia. Peter has a cabin around here," Mrs. Hughes continued. "Why isn't he writing this?"

"I don't know. May he's too busy editing." I replied. "So, you know the Johnstons?" I asked the hostess.

"Not well. My name is Lucinda Hughes. What is yours?"

"Robert Chappell. Glad to meet you."

Lucinda wore a wedding ring.

"The Johnstons are a lively family, aren't they?" I asked Mrs. Hughes.

"Lively? I'm not sure what you mean."

"They got thrown out of here a couple weeks ago. And, weren't they mixed up a while back in another murder?" I replied.

"I would hardly call the death of your son being mixed up in his murder. It is true that the dead man lost his wife a couple years ago," she acknowledged, "but it was never clear whether, as you put it, the family was mixed up with that death. Another man—her brother, in fact—was convicted of the crime. For a journalist, you're not careful with your words."

"Yes, I'm afraid you're right, Mrs. Hughes... Uh... The Johnstons? They're customers, or were?"

"They were asked to leave here a couple of weeks ago. But generally, they are quiet and well mannered. They are good enough customers, and regular. It was their older son who was at fault. The dead man. The parents have been eating here every Friday night for the past two or three years, and they had never presented any problems. I don't understand it, even now."

"What happened?" I asked.

"Nothing much. They had more to drink than usual, and it got away with them."

"Who was here?"

"The four of them, Mr. Chappell. Husband, wife, and the two sons. Your best sources for information about the Johnstons are the police. They've been here a couple times, and they've been all over Tilghman Island asking questions about the Johnstons."

"I plan to see the Johnstons. I just got here and haven't had a chance yet," I replied. "Also, there is only so much information that the police will let out to reporters—my article is about how the murder has affected the people who live here."

"He wants to give the murder a home for the city folks," the waitress volunteered.

Mrs. Hughes gave the waitress a funny look, and the waitress, looking at me, exclaimed, "That's what he told me!"

The hostess then looked at me without expression and said, "Excuse me, will you, Mr. Chappell. I'm glad you are enjoying your meal."

She left the room, traveling by way of where the oysters were being opened. She'd talked enough.

CHAPTER 5

Dogs of Tilghman

No chance to sleep late on Tuesday because, before dawn, wake from boats trafficking through the canal stirred the waters and *Jupiter*. On their way to harvest the sunken fields of the Bay, workboats motored past *Jupiter*, gently rocking her. Only a few generations before, some of the submerged fields the boats motored to had produced tobacco, corn, and like crops. Now claimed by the Bay, these hidden fields yielded crabs, oysters, and clams, depending on which bed you floated above. I sought my own harvest, preparing for the day by eating a milk, cereal, and sugar breakfast at *Jupiter*'s cabin table.

The gas station at the docks across the canal remained closed. A few stark lights there emphasized how lonely the station appeared in the darkness that first light would soon dissolve. At a distance, a traveler could think the lights of the station a sign of hope and assistance; up close, the lights could be as frustrating as a false promise. I would have to go to the station when it opened; it was a logical place to ask about renting a used car, maybe some old junker. Also, a description published in Easton Maryland's *Star Democrat* about Earl Johnston's murder supported waitress Betsy's account; it might be the station where Johnston's body had been found. If so, there might be a few questions to ask about the discovery.

I had time enough for a walk. A few blocks south of the drawbridge, the town of Tilghman spread out. One- and two-story houses here and there lined the few and casual streets of the town. No mansions on them. These were streets that, like ribs from a fish-fossil, some broken, reached out from the backbone of the main road, and many of them anyway went to the shores of the peninsula.

You take a small chance by walking at dawn in a small town. A chance that a tree might fall over on you out of nowhere. Or a dog might bite you. Dogs of a town, if it's the right sort of town, from one yard to another announce your progress, each dog along your route keeping alive the message of your coming. The dogs of Tilghman, however, were in poor voice that morning, for only a few of them made the effort, and only a couple of them coming to the road to offer a challenge in person.

On half alert, I had slept uneasily in case someone else from the darkness might appear again and attack. With daylight, no shadow remained menacing enough to cloth an assassin; so, my caution began to relax even in this land of strangers. Every time I wondered why anyone would have it in for me, only one answer came up: I didn't know. I had made a few enemies, but none of them were mortal. Maybe I had missed a bet, and I was being stalked by some quiet, overlooked grudge from the past? If only I could go straight to the source, crack it, and extract the right answers. There being no quick and dirty way of finding why the assault took place (barring a stroke of good luck), I had to proceed with care. I had to know at least a little about the territory I was entering.

My walk ended at the main road of the town and island, near a small country store. It was an old-time store, lacking frills in design—a one-story frame building, once painted white, now a mottled gray with age. The looks of the place fitted in with the decor of the town. Standing in front of it, I could see up the road, the drawbridge for the Narrows lying a quarter mile north. The store being open in that gray dawn, I walked in. A young man behind the counter asked, "Can I help you, mister? Raw eggs for breakfast? Hens just laid them. Still warm from the nest. Call me Alf."

"No. Thanks, Alf. Already ate. I'm just after some information."

"That's one thing that's not sold here," he said with a smile.

I stood for a moment, looking at a shelf stocked with Wheaties, Rice Chex, and like cereals, and not saying anything.

"The information's for free," the grocer continued. "What are you after?"

I explained my hunt for facts and opinion about the Johnston family for my maybe article and asked what he thought about the murder of Earl Johnston.

"There's been a lot of talk about it around here. Far as I can tell, people hope it will straighten things out, bring some peace," he responded.

"Why do you say that?"

"Earl was trouble, partly because he carried a lot of hard feelings and hates. A good many people also think he was behind burglaries locally. In the years that the Johnston family has lived in these parts, there have been people who disappeared in the middle of the night and were never heard from since. Two people anyway. No proof of murder, but..."

"That's pretty serious," I said. "What did the police do?"

"They looked around. At one time, there was a trial over his wife's death. The thing you've got to remember about Earl is that he was a midnight rambler. That was his finest hour. He loved to be out and about when nice folks is in bed."

"What about his wife's death?" I asked.

"I was coming to that. That's what the trial was all about, his comings and goings. I don't think anything ever did really shake out in terms of justice being done. There was a fellow—he looked a little like you—that was convicted of the murder, and maybe he did do it," Alf said. "Come to think of it, someone else was convicted of her murder. Someone in the victim's family."

"Wasn't me. I'm from the Western Shore."

"It's hard to tell. Maybe somebody with a grudge against Earl took it out against his wife. But, judging from the gossip around here, a good many people thought it just like Earl to frame another man for something he had done."

"Who's the man who looked like me?"

"It's not a close likeness, mister. More like a family resemblance. His name is Terence Markus, if he's still alive. Haven't heard anything about him since he went to prison. He's local. Not much good, but better than Earl. He hung around Earl for a while. You're not a Markus, are you?"

"No. I don't know anybody by that name. Where do the Markuses live?"

"Live? Don't know. The whole family moved away, out to California or someplace, after the trial."

A little old lady came in and called for eggs, butter, and bread. She complained that one of her teeth was bothering her and asked if the police had been by again about the murder. The grocer said no. Then he looked at me and asked my name, and when I told him, he, in a repeat performance, asked me to call him Alf. He then introduced me and my project to the old lady, Miss Gilden. My hunch was that she probably devoted her life to knowing what was going on in her community, whether in plain sight and worth repeating to the informed and uninformed, or out of sight and worth keeping within her circles. For my benefit and perhaps for community togetherness as well as for his curiosity, Alf asked what she thought of the murder.

"It was bloody. That's what I heard. So many knife wounds in him it was hard to see who it was. A maniac did it, I'm sure. My cousin's husband was with the ambulance that took Earl away. Imagine finding him by the gas station. Of all the places!"

"What does the Johnston family think of the murder?" I asked.

"The same as any family would. They're normal, even if Earl wasn't," the old lady said.

"A lot of people don't agree with you, Miss Gilden," the grocer said.

"They never have agreed with me, Alf," she countered. "You know Earl was a lightning rod to that family. They ended up with the trouble that Earl brought. Just because they showed off their money more than they should have doesn't make them bad. You're sore, Alf, because they drive all the way to Easton and the large grocery stores rather than buy from you."

"Miss Gilden…" the grocer faltered.

"I feel sorry for them," she continued. "It is God's shame the way people around here have treated the Johnstons because of Earl," she concluded, picking up her bag of groceries and walking out the door.

"That lady who just left is Miss Gilden," Alf said to me. "She represents local history here. She has a reputation as a good catch at one time for the suitors she had attracted… until only a few years ago. Too proud to marry young. But, she's also a nice enough person. Earl Johnston once killed a dog she had. It ran at his motorcycle while he was riding it a while back. He got off, picked up a stick, and went after the dog. The dog had more heart than brains and lost both when Earl took after him. Even so, Miss Gilden stands up for the Johnston family. One of the few around here that does."

Coming out from the store and turning toward the bridge, I saw Miss Gilden ahead of me. In a minute or so, I had caught up with her and was walking past when she said, "Young man, you can't leave those poor people alone, can you?"

"No, ma'am. It's how I earn my living."

"In that case, instead of nibbling at the edges of it, you should go see them. Get their views of the tragedy. The Johnstons are not a nest for the Devil like some think."

"I'm going to do that, but they will probably not welcome another stranger with questions."

"You're right, young man."

I could start to knock on doors and canvass the town for gossip about the Johnstons, or I could take Miss Gilden's advice. Her advice meant getting to the marrow of my search; it was time to go to the gas station just beyond the bridge. Maybe I could rent a car or find out where I could rent one. It was clear that, sooner or later, I would have to visit the Johnston family to find out what we might have of mutual interest. How to approach the Johnstons posed a problem—to phone first, or head right in and, cold turkey, say, "Hi there! I'm a reporter from the big-time newspaper, about to flatter you with my presence and make a celebrity out of you. Tell me your story. I'll print it. And, maybe the printing of your story will plow up the earth that hides the causes of your son's death, and the killers of your son will be identified by some shy observer of your son's death, and those killers will be caught." Well, maybe the exact wording needed a polish.

Phoning the Johnstons was too risky. Too much chance of my going up against a shook-up situation, kept stirred by the fatigue and the grief of the Johnstons, who probably had suffered too much contact with police on an unsociable basis. Who knows what reporters had gotten to them before me and fouled the nest with hard and pushy questions that were none of the public's business but that represented popular interest in sorrow and soap (the joy of living, the grief of others)? I figured the best way to proceed was to go unannounced in person and take my chances, giving me the advantage of surprise. It would be harder for them to turn me down to my face than over the phone, assuming my face did not provoke another attack. I did have an open, approachable face. If things got rough, I had the dodge of, "The newspaper knows I'm here. So do the police."

After walking back to the Narrows and the drawbridge, I checked *Jupiter*. She was fine. Then I walked across the bridge to the gas station and garage, approached an attendant, and asked where I could rent a car after explaining my search for news.

"You'd better see them while you can." The attendant was a big, red-haired albino who deserved to be called "Red" because of his hair and the color of his face. He stood a couple of inches taller than me, making him tall enough to have played basketball in high school, which couldn't have been more than a year or two before our meeting.

"What's up?" I asked.

"Don't know how much longer the Johnstons are going to be around here."

"Why?"

"They've got a lot of enemies because of their son, Earl. Do you know Earl?"

"Briefly," I replied.

"Earl's not around anymore. He's moved to another world, as I guess you know. Now that there's no one to protect his parents, Carney and Mae, some old scores will likely be settled, I expect."

Nothing like the assumed authority of the young, I thought. "Carney can probably take care of himself," I said.

"You speaking from experience? Their other son's moved away."

"Nestor?"

"Yea. He's working on the Western shore."

"You know that? That's what I heard."

"Yes."

"At a boat yard?"

"Yes."

"That your boat over there?" Red asked.

"Yes."

"Saw you on it. You're a newspaper reporter? Your business is looking into other people's business?"

"Yes. I'm a curiosity feeder. Keep the public informed."

"Slow way to get a newspaper story, isn't it? The way you're going at it."

"What do you know about getting a newspaper story?" I asked Red.

"Not much. Just checking you out."

"Good work requires the time available for it. Also, it depends on what kind of story you're after and how you get it. Earl Johnston's body was found near here, wasn't it?"

"Could be. There's not much of a story in that. I found him when I came in to open the place. That's it. End of story. Goodbye."

"Goodbye to $20.00?"

"You paying for information?"

"I want to rent a car."

"Took a chance coming over here with your boat, hoping to get a car, didn't you?"

"You're spunky for a kid, aren't you?"

"What do you mean by 'spunky?'"

"Where's the owner of this station?"

Red paused before answering, "It won't do you any good talking to him. We don't rent cars here. I'm not trying to give you a hard time, mister. We've had problems around here with lending things to strangers and not getting them back."

"Suit yourself. Somebody around here can use twenty bucks."

"You'd only have the car for a couple hours before I'd need it back."

"That's time enough."

"Okay… there's a junker out back I'll rent you. Just wanted to test you."

~

Red considered my boat as security for his car, which made me uneasy because he looked like the type who would close the station and take off on the boat for the day or longer. He probably did not know much about how to manage a sailboat. And, I probably wouldn't be long if Betsy was right and the Johnston place lay only a couple of miles up the Neck.

She was right. White letters of "Johnston" against a black aluminum, miniature Quonset hut mail box identified the address. It was off Harris Creek. Being close to the Creek, the Johnston place offered the possibility of my return later by boat. The Johnston house stood in a clearing, well enough away from the surrounding woods so that the folks at home would not have to worry about Virginia creeper coming out of the woods and burying their house in green. Not that any great loss would come to humanity if the creeper did come. The house was a Cape Cod frame, recently painted white, sheltered by a red, shingled roof. The grounds were likewise nothing fancy but well maintained: cut lawn and no potholes in the dirt and gravel road to it.

No one was at home, so I walked around the place. Peace and quiet hung around the place, suggesting again that orderly folks lived there. The Johnstons had a short dock, at the end of which was tied a workboat, probably the one that Earl had used to follow me. It looked like it anyway. Up close, you could see that the boat was in rough shape, needing paint and care. I walked down to the dock to look it over. The remains of a small, dried, red-brown puddle dyed the starboard gunwale of the boat. Dried blood of a person or fish? I could not tell.

An old pickup truck drove into the yard and stopped next to my car. Two men got out, both as rough-looking as their vehicle, a study in the success of rust and the frailty of steel. Both men wore work clothes, jeans, and flannel shirts appropriate for an autumn day, open enough at the neck to show the world where the brown-red from the sun met the sheltered, crab belly white on their skins. They were solid men. They carried themselves with some arrogance, as if they would not be crossed, much less be taken lightly. The shorter of the two spoke to me as they approached:

"You've got Red Farrell's junker, mister," he said, gruffly.

"I'm renting it from him."

"It's my car, not Red's," shorty remarked, continuing. "But, no problem. I let him earn a little money on the side, even if it's my money. You wouldn't be a Markus, would you?" he asked.

"No. I've already been asked that. I don't even know the family, though I'm told there's a resemblance."

"You sightseeing?" the short one continued.

"You could say that," I replied, and continued by explaining my search for a feature story. "What are you all here for?" I asked, ending my piece.

"Come to pick up my boat, my brother and me. It's been stole for a week. Friend found it this morning, so we've come to take what is ours," he replied.

"Did Earl take it?" I asked.

"Looks like it, and I should have known it," the short one replied.

"Looks also like he chewed it up a little," the tall man joined in.

"Where are the Johnstons?" I asked.

"Probably at the funeral, Earl's funeral," the short one replied. "Carney knows we're here."

"When do you think they'll be back?" I asked.

"Never, I hope," the short one said with a harsh laugh.

"What do you all think of Earl's murder? Does it make any difference?" I asked the short one.

"What's it to you?" the short one asked. "You from the newspapers?"

"Yes. I work out of Annapolis."

"So, what do I think of Johnston's murder? Some think it was overdue, or some punishment was. If they was a right and a wrong way to do something, Earl would try to ride the difference. The trouble was, he kept on losing his balance and falling on the wrong side. Earl was crazy. He knew we would come looking for our boat here, sooner or later. We'd had trouble before. It was just a matter of time. He took the boat because he thought he needed it more than anyone else did, and he liked to stick it to people."

"Why'd he need it?" I asked.

"Oh… you don't know much about this country. Earl probably wanted to go into business for himself," said the short one, who was doing most of the talking.

"I need your names for the article," I said.

"Just call us the Whittier brothers," the short one replied. "I'm Turk. He's Marvin, but we call him 'Marv.'"

They walked to the boat while I stood and watched, reflecting that interviewing people about the dead was standard enough newspaper procedure, sometimes ghoulish. They inspected the boat. The small one started the motor.

"Hey, Turk!" the short one called out. "Earl spilled something on the side here. Looks like blood."

I walked over for a closer look. A brown stain covered a part of the deck, where as best I could tell, Earl had landed when he had jumped from my boat. Turk, who had gone to the small cabin, came over to see for himself.

He said, "Earl was a real slob. Who knows whose blood it is? Maybe it's Earl's. Maybe fish! Marv! The boat's okay. You take the truck back. I'll take the boat for some gas. See you tonight."

Marv walked back to the truck and drove off while I played good scout and cast off the dock lines onto the boat and watched it head east to the center of the channel and then turn south where the open waters of the Choptank River were. The only thing left for me to do, as the dock and homestead grew silent, was to figure out my next move. I had to return the car by

4:00 p.m. when Red got off work. After that, I could wait until the next morning, and with the following wind of a fresh day, start on my interview with the Johnston survivors. Or, I could find some way to return in the evening and take my chances with them.

I returned the car before Red got off work. *Jupiter*'s being in the same spot I left her in Red's care impressed me. The goodwill from my proven honesty prompted Red to phone a friend of his who had an extra car and who was willing to rent it to me for $20.00 a day, minimum of two days, and to allow me to drop the extra car off with Red when I was through. Red said he was going to have to use the junker, which I had gotten to like.

While Red and I waited for his friend to deliver the extra car, I asked him a couple more questions about how he found Earl's body; but he said he had talked enough about it to the police and did not want to say anymore. Red's silence allowed me to think about how the Johnstons had proved to be no-shows. When would be the best time to see them? Given their dead son's behavior, they were likely to be shy folk, and there was no way of telling whether it would be a good idea to try and talk to them about their son on the day of his funeral. So, after my car appeared, I gave into an impulse to eat supper early and think over the matter some more. I drove across the bridge to the Half Way House.

History repeated part of itself again. Mrs. Hughes escorted me to my table so that I would not get hurt or lost on the way. My waitress of the previous night appeared again and, in time, so did the same meal. It still tasted good. Her friendliness proved the value of a big tip and her clear recollection of it. She improved on her boss's earlier introduction saying that her full name was Betsy Winter, and I told her my name. Nice to meet you. Business being slow again, following the summer hurry-up, she tarried and asked:

"How's the article coming along?"

"Almost finished the research on it."

"Are you going to quote me?"

"I'm not sure."

"Did you find a home for the murder?"

"I spoke out of turn last night. I shouldn't have said that."

"You really caught me by surprise, Mr. Chappell."

"Please call me Robert."

"You surprised Mrs. Hughes too, I think. What did you find out?"

"The Johnstons don't have many friends around here. Almost everyone I've talked to didn't like murder, but also did not mind seeing Earl get his."

"Don't be surprised if the Johnstons are asked to leave."

"Who would do the asking?"

"A group of concerned citizens. Isn't that how the newspapers would put it?"

"You mean vigilantes?"

"More or less. Earl isn't around anymore to pay his own debts."

"You seem young to know about such things."

"We grow up quickly around here, Robert."

With that, she turned smoothly and, for a moment, her skirt taut against her leg showed me a well-turned thigh as she strode toward the kitchen. Wonders of the flesh; my, how she had improved in a day. Could she and Red, the gas station attendant, have attended the same high school? She seemed older than I first thought.

Betsy the waitress got me to thinking of Edith, my hot-and-cold girlfriend, part-time feminist, and full-time free spirit. Edith believed in long vacations from "relationships." So, we had been seeing each other several times a week for a month or two at a stretch, and then she would disappear for a while before reappearing. She was the opposite of my ex-wife, who remained a woman fiercely devoted to being a pillar of the community, and committed to duty and the proper discharge of responsibility. My wife had also suffered spells of the unforgiving, which developed so that she got fed up with the life she led with me. A mistress of silent, unforgiving grudges leavened by forgiveness and abiding loyalty underneath it all, or so I thought until the divorce. The chaos of my schedule and my lax attitude toward non-business appointments offered her a change of pace she did not want, after the novelty had worn off. For my part, before the chafe set in, I liked the comfort of an externally-imposed routine while being lax in observing it.

Anyway, it was as good enough time as any to phone Edith and see if the attack had left any after effects on her. Did she have any second thoughts about her talk with the police. Also, had she had resumed freelancing for other social life? Her phone rang and rang. No answer.

The Johnstons would probably be just as likely to talk after the funeral and get some of the grief out of their systems as they would any time in the next couple of days. So, why not try them again?

While driving back to the Johnstons in the evening light, I realized that the attempt on my life and the tension and suspense that followed could skew my judgment. The Johnstons, sensitized by the news story of Earl's death, might doubt my claim to be a newspaperman. How personal can you get? I was, after all, a stranger, and Carney was an old hand at making his way through the world. Or, the Johnstons might mistake me for a Marcus, whoever they were, and be hostile, their emotions heightened by the day's events. There was little I could do if those difficulties arose except to improvise and trust to luck.

My mood passed quickly. Who knows where the hands of my destiny had been? I was too riled up and apprehensive to let things ride as they had been. All things considered, I thought it best to watch the Johnstons from a distance, if possible, and see how they moved. See if they had any of their dead son's violence.

See if as a couple they screamed or brooded, or behaved somewhere in between, thereby giving a clue of the genetics that formed their dead son.

A quarter of a mile or so before the dirt driveway that led to the Johnston place, I pulled off the road next to a stand of trees, as if I were an unarmed hunter off to scout the neighborhood supply of squirrels and rabbits. I walked to the Johnston road, looked down it, saw no one, and then continued walking further for fifty yards or so, before turning into the woods and heading cross country for the house. I walked a true course by keeping the sun to my back. All the junk foliage in my path, creepers and other vines, and thickets of brambles (all a paradise for ticks), made me pay for my caution. It's hard to trust southern woods, hard to know where to step, because of the copperhead snakes about. Give me the spare, rocky woods of the Pacific Northwest and their rattlesnakes.

I inclined to the right, to get closer to the Johnston driveway. The sound of a car passing on the main road reminded me that vigilantes might be afoot when it grew dark, if Betsy had told me the truth, so I had to watch the time. After a few minutes, I saw the woods thin out ahead, revealing the Johnston house.

This time someone was home, judging from the late model Mercedes Benz estate wagon next to the house. It was time to wait for the cover of darkness before proceeding further, and to take a chance that I would leave before the vigilantes arrived, again assuming that Betsy was right. Night took its own good time in coming. Eventually, someone turned on lights in the

Johnston house. I waited another hour before making my move.

You couldn't see much through the windows, other than a movement now and then behind lace curtains. I would have to get closer. That meant crossing the yard without anything to hide behind. If I should be discovered in the yard, there would be no place to run to, unless it was in the brush a few yards away, down by the water and Harris Creek itself. To make the most of little, I crept in the underbrush around the clearing until I got near the water. After that, it was time once again to crawl through one more infiltration course, this time without benefit of exploding dynamite, machine gun fire with tracer bullets a couple feet up, and the distractions of barbed wire, a field pack, a carbine, and a desire for peace and quiet at the end of a long day. I got down on my belly and on my way.

When I finally reached the house and was inching toward a view through a lighted window, a large dog began to bark inside the house. I froze. I had forgotten to plan for this possibility. The damn dog continued to bark. This was no time for chance, so I crouched and began to run for the water. Floodlights came on; the whole yard had been wired. Someone opened the back door. I glanced back. A German shepherd bounded out the door, down the steps, and after me. Behind the dog was an old man with a shotgun. I reached the water a few lengths ahead of the dog, heard a shot ring out, and felt a sting in my right shoulder. I dove. The water proved to be deep enough for me to swim under the surface. I came up for air, dove under again and again until I had reached a fair distance from the shore.

When I reached the shore downstream from the Johnston place, I was exhausted from my narrow escape and from swimming with my clothes and shoes on. I began to shiver. There was an old, rutted road that led back to the main road, and it took only a few minutes to make my way back to the car, and a few minutes more to return to *Jupiter*. There, I checked the sting in my shoulder, and found that it came from where a shotgun pellet had winged me. Perspective sometimes comes late to me, as it did on this occasion when the full stupidity of the chances I had taken became apparent. Once again, my obsession with rush and haste to get things done worked against me.

The lights of the Half Way House restaurant remained bright enough to help guide me when boarding *Jupiter*. If I changed clothes quickly enough and got in to the restaurant before closing time, that would give someone else a chance to make coffee, but I never made it. I had put on a pair of dry pants and was dressing the wound on my shoulders when I heard a woman call out my name from outside the boat.

"Betsy?" I responded.

"Yes. I just got off work and wondered how the story was going. Can I come on your boat?"

"Sure."

She came down into the main cabin, looked at me with

surprise, and asked, "What happened to you?"

I hadn't put on a shirt and, with my wound showing and my hair still wet, I must have looked rough. "Didn't watch my step along the canal. I fell into the water."

"How'd you hurt yourself?"

"I hit something. I'm not sure what."

"Let me take a look at it. I studied nursing for a while."

After a brief examination, she said, "It doesn't look like a normal wound. Did you get shot?"

"There are hazards to wandering about at night. It was dumb. I wanted to clear my head and I had an accident. Nobody shot me."

Betsy insisted on helping me with applying dressing and iodine I had stored on *Jupiter* for emergencies, and used a firm, persuasive touch that began to overcome the sting from the wound. She seemed to take a more than passing interest in patching me up; she showed a tenderness that could turn volatile. In those few moments when she patched me up, the two of us reached the uncharted waters that men and women often travel when they have the time and privacy to see if there is anything more between them than season's greetings. At first, the mood can go anywhere. But, one touch leads to another touch and then to a third. Silent greetings grow in number and in warmth.

"There's a chill," I said, after she had finished with the bandage. "I'll close the hatches and make it more comfortable in here."

"How's the story coming along," she asked again as I worked at the task at hand.

"Fine. I'll probably finish my research for it tomorrow," not sure when I would write the story, much less which angle to take in telling it.

"Then you'll write it?"

"Yes."

"How come you don't have a notebook like other reporters?"

"I do. I don't use it often because I've got a good memory. It depends on my mood and the story I've got to write."

Betsy paused before asking, "When will you be leaving?"

"Probably tomorrow. But I'll be back. I've been here before."

"I've never seen you."

"You weren't looking."

She laughed. By now I had finished closing *Jupiter* against the chilly night air, and the boat lay snug and quiet.

"How about something to drink? Something to take away the pain of the day?" I asked.

"What do you recommend?"

"Wine. It's kind to your system."

"I'll take a beer. I love to be waited on," she said, smiling. She was no innocent. I sized Betsy up as having years of knowledge about people, knowledge hidden by her youth. She was a natural, a very young natural. Just shy of jailbait. Even so, her youth put me on the alert.

Light from the kerosene lamp caught the sheen of the auburn in her hair, young autumn. I took out two beers from the cooler. I opened them both and handed one to Betsy. She leaned back against the seat, her legs up on it, and her skirt high enough to reveal one shapely leg crossed over the other, with a plump, rounded knee well displayed on top. I sat next to her and, with mixed feelings, put my arm around her. She nested. We exchanged biographies. She was home grown in a small town near Tilghman Island. She would wait tables until something better came along, which she hoped would be soon.

At one point she laughed at something I said and let her hand drop lightly on my thigh. She deserved a kiss for that and got one, and another, and yet another. I did not take much to move from there to the main course, served forward in the v-berth. No shyness with Betsy. She was a healthy country girl who knew her way around.

After our love knot came undone, she went to sleep while I lay awake listening to the sounds of the water and of the night. I rose and went on deck to check the boat and the lines that held her fast. To the north there was a glow in the sky, as if from a large fire. Who was there? What was changing in the heat of the fire? Wood to ash? Life to death? Anyway, all lay secure on *Jupiter* under a harvest moon.

A new line guide, the glue for it still warm, sat on the tip of one of my fishing rods. I'd been repairing the rod in the calm of the dawn, when Betsy made her way from the V berth to join me.

The light of the morning restored a few of Betsy's angles that, the night before, had been curves, but she nevertheless retained her choice parts.

"Morning stranger," I said. "You ready to buy the boat now?"

She smiled and said, "Where's the coffee?"

"I hoped that you'd make it. You're the one in the food business."

"What happened to last night's romance?" she asked.

"Would you like it served this morning?" I said, not realizing what I was letting myself in for.

"Just try me," she responded, and adopted a provocative pose. Lacking wit, considering the problems that awaited me later in the day, and not being in the mood to respond appropriately to Betsy's challenge, I said nothing, but started to make coffee and to cook bacon and eggs, the old standby.

"How about some company on your way back home?" Betsy asked. "You won't turn me down on that, will you?"

"No. But, I'm not ready for marriage."

"How about a live-in maid?"

"Not right now. I've got to move around a lot, and that would mean lonely nights for you."

"You've got another lady?"

"Kind of."

"I should have known it. You don't think much of me," Betsy continued.

"I like you. It's just that I've been this route before."

"Burned, right? Divorced?"

"Yep."

"How come there are so many like you around?"

"How about setting the table?"

She set the table, reluctantly, tired of waiting on tables. We ate in silence until I asked where she lived. Sometimes in a room she rented, she replied, sometimes with her boyfriend. More silence. I asked, "Is Red Farrell your boyfriend?"

"No," she answered with an edge in her voice. "But my boyfriend's a friend of Red."

"Your boyfriend's going to come looking for you, isn't he?"

"Maybe, but I don't think so. He was going out with Red and the boys last night."

"Poker and beer?"

"Not likely," she replied with a trace of anger. It seemed to be anger not at me but towards her boyfriend. "He was with a group of concerned citizens," she continued.

"Did they go where I think they went?"

"That's what they planned on. I shouldn't have told you this. Please don't put this in your article, or it will be good bye for me."

"He'd kill you?"

"He'd beat the hell out of me."

"Again?"

"Yes."

"That's why you want to get away from here? Improved living conditions?"

"Yes. There's no future here for me. It's been fun. It's time to split. If my boyfriend comes by here, don't tell him anything, will you?"

"No. I don't even know what his name is or what he looks like."

"Good."

"You can come back with me, if you want. I'll find some place to put you up."

"Thanks, but no thanks. I wouldn't want to get in between you and your old lady."

After closing *Jupiter* again, I drove to the Johnston place to see what the concerned citizens had accomplished. The house had burned to the ground. A state police car sat parked near the site of the citizens' "offering." And, near the Johnston's pier a middle-aged man in a poorly fitting, garish sports coat and mouse-colored pants stood, looking at me. He asked what he could do for me when I approached. I told him my reporter story and embellished it to bring it up to date.

Identifying himself as Detective Schand of the Maryland State Police, he spoke with polite reluctance; one more talk for him with a nosey reporter. Time spent to no good purpose. After a while, though, again he opened a little and, with few words and no emotion, disclosed that neighbors had heard a couple of shots early in the evening. Later, the Johnstons had been seen driving toward Easton. Shortly before midnight, fire broke out in the Johnston house. The fire department arrived at 12:28 a.m. to find most of the house burned. No bodies found. Arson suspected.

"Any way of telling where the Johnstons went?" I asked.

"Could be, but I don't know it. Maybe they'll be back. Maybe they won't."

"Is there any evidence," I asked, "to connect the fire with the murder? Earl's murder?"

"Not that I know of, but it's a thought," he responded.

"I haven't had a chance to phone back to my paper. Was there any other violence around here last night?"

"The violence got to two locals, a mile or so from here. Their names, Marvin and Turk Whittier. They were shot at. Marvin's in the hospital with shotgun pellets in the gut. The Whittiers say they don't know who did it," the detective said.

"Any connection with the fire?"

"Not that I could prove. Marvin and Turk used to hang out with Earl Johnston, the deceased. Then, they fell out. I don't know whether there's a feud going on here or not."

"Were the Whittier brothers questioned about Earl's murder?" I asked.

"I believe so, but nothing turned up."

"What about the Markus family?"

"They would probably be in this thing too, if they still lived here."

"About Earl's murder, could a couple of people have killed

him? I saw the pictures of the corpse. He had been badly cut up."

"That's putting it mildly," the detective said.

"Why was Earl killed?"

"Why not? Apart from that, no comment for now."

It was time to whistle in the dark, return the car, and think about sailing home. With the Johnstons taking to the tall grass, what could I do? Nothing but go home and take my chances. With luck, Edith would be available again. I drove the car back to the gas station and to Red, who had said I could leave the car with him. As I approached him, he said:

"Get your story? See the ashes? I saw you drive up there this morning as I was opening this place up."

"Yes, I saw it. What happened?"

"Big fire," Red replied. "That's all I know. You get anything else you were after?"

"Such as?"

"Betsy."

"What do you mean?"

"I also saw Betsy get off your boat this morning."

"So?"

"Her boyfriend won't like it. He's my friend. I don't like it."

"All of us have something we don't like, including me."

"What don't you like?" Red said, moving closer toward me

as if to get ready for a fight.

"The show I watched at the Johnston place, last night. I staked it out and watched you and the others torch it."

"You left Betsy to watch us? Bull shit!"

"I can get laid anytime I want. I don't have to travel over here for a piece of ass." Time to talk nasty for a nasty situation. I continued: "I did have to travel over here to get the story I wanted. Betsy spent the night on *Jupiter* because she had no place to go and feel safe. Your friend likes to beat her up, and she doesn't like to get beaten up." What could I lose with a bluff?

Red asked, "Why'd you go back to the Johnstons this morning?"

"To see if I'd missed anything last night."

"You going to write this up or go the police?"

"It depends. Keep your mouth shut. Forget about saying anything to your friend about Betsy, and relax. And, I can write the story without saying anything about the fire. And, the cops do well enough on their own."

Without saying anything, Red turned to walk into the station, while I headed to the bridge and the Half Way House. There I ate lunch. Even though I told Betsy that Red had seen her leave *Jupiter*, she said indifferently only that it was "too bad." I returned to *Jupiter* for the sail home.

As I walked down the low hill that led to the canal, a small, open aluminum craft with an outboard motor made its way East, toward the Choptank and away from the Bay. A large man with red hair in this small craft steered it, while another, shorter man, sat forward. Looked like Red but my sighting proved to be too brief to be sure.

Jupiter lay low in the water. The lock on the main cabin hatch was broken. I went below and found water just over the floor of the main cabin, up to the engine's oil pan, and a couple inches short of the batteries. I heard a gurgling, and frantically traced it as coming from a seacock mounted inside a galley cabinet and normally used for protecting the through hull water lines for the sink. The kitchen drain hose had been removed from the seacock, and the valve left open, and water gushed into the boat. The danger ended when I closed the valve to stop the influx of water. For the next half an hour I pumped out the boat by electric pump and by a hand pump, and then reinstalled the hose. A little while longer and I would have lost *Jupiter*.

I thought I'd gotten away with my bluff with Red. Now, Red's message, and maybe that of his "wronged" friend, was clear enough: for every pleasure there's a little pain. There was, however, another possibility: the "first cause" of my recent troubles endured, and that I was no closer to safety than I had been when Earl Johnston had boarded my boat. What lay behind his attack, one cause or two, or maybe more? Old grievances can be slow to die. I had none to speak of.

CHAPTER 6

Near Miss on Mill Swamp Road

By noon, *Jupiter* lay a mile or so off Knapp's Narrows and still a couple miles south of Poplar Island. It was partly cloudy. Wind sauntered from the south, five knots at best when it got a move on. The wind from the south and a friendly tide would determine when *Jupiter* would return to Galesville. Of course, a miscalculated approach of night might persuade me to start the motor and finish the journey under power. The outward route back home seemed the best way to go, which meant sailing for much of the distance in the main shipping channel up the middle of the Bay. Given the wind from the south, Poplar Island would hardly block the wind. The chance that the Island would block much wind remained small anyway, given the shortage of trees and their low height on the island. Also, so far as my safety was concerned, little if any danger remained of Red and friends finding me if they had decided (for the love of honor and Betsy) to take out after me in a motorboat. *Jupiter* had moved too far out from shore to be easily found. That unfulfilled possibility kept me alert.

As the afternoon matured, the sky clouded over and the weather turned undecided whether to blow and rain or be calm and let the sunshine. Mother Nature awarded me a sampler of each kind of weather. There weren't many boats out, it being a weekday. When the wind rose, I would by habit tense for the unexpected and the unlikely—high winds, for example. Winds on the Bay a few times a year during the temperate months descend from a haze in the West. Such winds start from nothing and, within a few minutes, reach the force of a whole gale or even a storm. Nothing to mess with on the water, much less on land. Sometimes the winds come from a thunderhead's microburst. On land, such winds pummel buildings, and break trees and even uproot them. At sea, where vast depths prevail beneath the surface, winds of this sort stir up massive waves. Foam blows in dense streaks, allowing little visibility. In Chesapeake Bay, large waves find little footing, the waters being so shallow; waters that, whipped by a squall, become confused. That can happen on rare occasions when high winds, like a great beast in a blood lust, tear into any small prey or craft without hope of shelter.

There are other events to watch for as well. On a day like this, with a haze dissolving the horizon and then obscuring closer views and with squalls dropping rain curtains here and there, freighters and tankers go on the prowl. They sound loud, base horns. Should there be fog, the sound becomes confusing, and it is hard to tell from where such warnings come. Notwithstanding the miracle of radar, you can still be run over on the Bay, perhaps because the watch or pilot on a freighter missed your blip on the screen, or perhaps in the dark of the moon, the officer in charge wanted to prepare for a long voyage as the ancients did with a little raw meat. A sacrifice to the Gods—the age of human sacrifice still being with us. Missions of determined business intent send these freighters on their way. Responding to the high purpose of maintaining the speed required by the profit a ship can turn and, considering that freighters take a mile or two to change course regardless of what lies before them, the pilots, crews, officers, and captains press on. They respond to the high purpose of maintaining the speed required by the profit a ship must earn, considering that freighters take a mile or two to change course regardless of what lies before them.

At Galesville in the dusk, I secured Jupiter in her slip at the Rudd Yard and used the yard pay phone to contact Edith again to see how she was doing. Again, no answer. Given the way in which violence had struck Edith and me out of darkness, I worried once again about having missed something, and about some hidden danger still present. I tried to put away my worries by saying to myself that fatigue was making me uneasy.

I could drive to Edith's apartment and wait there on the chance that she might return home from her social wanderings. She might not, however, return home for days. Or, I could put off the worry by staying put on *Jupiter* for the night, phoning her when I thought of it, and letting fears nibble at me like mosquitos. Too much effort to return to my land nest. My best idea. Clean up in the showers at the Rudd Yard, and then go to the Clam Pier. There I would freshen up still more with a gin and tonic and, with my friend Peter (well acquainted with social news of the Middle Chesapeake Bay), talk about the Johnstons and my personal concerns about Edith.

It was Wednesday night, three nights after the assault on me and Earl's murder. Rumors find bars and restaurants a natural roost. The Clam Pier, however, offered little chance for gossip because none of the regulars was there. Business was slow. In the cool of the evening, I sat at a table in a room with a close view of the restaurant's docks. Nothing fancy about the décor of room, protected from the outside world by huge, wire screens in place of glass. Large spider webs in the upper corners of the screens gave the room a spooky feel when you looked at them.

While Peter Cave made a few telephone calls, I was able to read the newspapers of the past couple of days, catching up on the news. These newspapers were available to me because Peter was a saver of them. I wrote for newspapers; he saved them —

newspapers, something we had in common, kind of. Peter was a kind man who liked the few journalists he knew and the short route they offered him to the world at large. He approached middle age with enough confidence to marry a pretty woman fifteen years his junior. She proved independent enough to be seldom seen at the restaurant.

None of the papers I read offered any further mention of the Earl Johnston investigation nor even of the fire at his parents' place. When Peter came around, he said that the grape vine offered no recent news about the Johnstons, not that they ever made the vine. He explained that, normally, he heard little about Eastern Shore people. However, he did know that a Johnston boy worked at Rudd's yard, a quiet fellow who minded his own business and who seldom spent his money needlessly, such as at a restaurant. The boy apparently lived by himself.

Peter had brought over a couple beers, on the house, by way of refreshing once again our long-standing friendship. I often ate at the Clam Pier, for good luck and for the convenience of it, before starting out for a cruise. Peter asked if there was any special reason for my hunt through the papers. I told him of Johnston's attack on me and my effort to find out why.

"Why didn't you ask me about this before you left for Tilghman?" he asked.

"I was all shook up. I wanted to get started quickly. I should have talked to you, but I just didn't think of it."

"You're lucky you didn't get shot or killed, Robert."

"I guess so. I've heard that there have been hard feelings,

even a feud, on Tilghman Island between what I understand to be the Johnstons, the Markus family, and the Whittiers," I said. "Do you know anything about that?"

"Not much. I wouldn't be surprised if Earl didn't have something to do with it. I knew him, but not well. A few months ago, Earl held up a restaurant in London Town, on the South River. He made a real name for himself over there. A smart lawyer got him off with probation."

"Is that how you knew him?"

"No. His wife… ex-wife… dead wife… worked as a waitress for a friend of mine in Annapolis. Her name was Cindy. She was a blue-collar social activist. Her program was to reform Earl. Why she had anything to do with him, I don't know. Probably animal magnetism. I didn't know her that well."

"How did she die?"

"Strange, the newspaper said. Maybe assault. It happened about a year and a half ago," Peter replied.

"Who did it?"

"I don't know. The jury, I think, convicted her brother, a guy named Terry Markus."

"Markus?"

"Yes. Earl told the court that he came home late one night and found Cindy dead. Terry's filleting knife was near the body. The police tried to shake Earl's story but couldn't, especially after Terry Markus confessed to the murder."

"Confessed?"

"Yes. There was a lot of comment at the time that the story

didn't hang together. But the conviction stood."

"What was Terry's motive supposed to be?" I asked.

"In his confession, he said he was just hard up for her. They never got along as kids. Sibling rivalry or something like that."

"And the police went along with this?"

"Them and the court. A crime of passion. What isn't?"

I shifted in my chair and asked, "How do you figure it out?"

"I didn't. I don't."

"Do you have any ideas about why Johnston attacked me?"

"No idea. Maybe it was your looks. Maybe he thought that you were a Markus who was up to something… come back for revenge. Maybe Earl wanted to make an impression on Edith, though I don't know that he ever met her. I'm just fishing."

"Edith doesn't know him. At least I don't think so. I don't see how she could."

"Well, Robert, she is a good looking, frail thing. Maybe he fell in love with her at first sight last week when you and him almost got into a fight here. Maybe he thought he could move in on you and take her away. I remember hearing something that he had done something like that with Cindy. Have you asked Edith?"

"No. I just assumed that Earl was after me, for whatever reason."

All this was enough to get me out of my chair and over to the payphone, where I dialed Ma Bell's wheel of fortune again, and again there was no answer at Edith's. When I mentioned my luck to Peter, he too did not know what to make of it. There was no telling what Edith was up to or where she was doing it. So, giving into the inevitable, I left the comfort of the Clam Pier to return to check Edith's condo and, if nothing turned up, leave a note of inquiry short of distress.

Edith and I had been seeing one another off and on for better than a year. We had met in Sea Girt, New Jersey, one weekend while I was getting away from it all and she was on a holiday from Annapolis. A one-night stand led to repeats and an off-and-on again friendship, with my traveling to Annapolis to see her, and she sometimes replying in kind to New Jersey. She proved to be good company in addition to great sex.

For all our compatibility, I did not know much about her. Only later did I learn that Edith was married on the road to divorce, which she had since obtained. Divorce presented a common interest for the two of us, the chief difference between us being that she saw her ex from time to time. But, more than that, while I had already sailed that course, she refused to discuss her voyage. Nor did she say anything about where she had been born and raised, where her family lived or even if she had one, and who else she saw, if anyone. Once, she mentioned having born a child who had died at birth. She resisted my curiosity, sensitive as she was about her past.

She made it clear that she treasured her privacy. Nevertheless, there was enough to her made public, minute by minute, to keep me occupied. To all appearances, she came by some of her money as a junior analyst for the National Security Agency, which required some restraint of talk. Now she was at loose ends; the agency had furloughed her, putting her commute to the Agency on hold for a bureaucratic solution. She appeared to enjoy other sources of income but would say nothing to me about what they were. Her tastes being expensive, she apparently had little walking-around money. The small, elegant condo that she rented in a small, elegant apartment building probably required Edith to practice conscientious budgeting—only a sometime talent for me.

She had contradictions to add to her allure. For instance, amid her apartment's good taste, she would occasionally hold forth about how she really did not like to collect material things and about how her needs were small. Edith said she liked me, or at least spent time with me, for sex and philosophical reasons: she wanted to see what "old money" (my inheritance) did to a person. She joked that I was a case study in morality. Though she saw no immediate sign that I had given my life over to decadence, she thought I would eventually do so, and she wanted to watch how decadence took over a person's life. Privately dismissing her estimate of my future, I would compliment her on what she did for my person, old money or not, for she was a charmer who balanced affection toward me with an underlying reserve.

What possibilities remained for following the origins of the attack on me and maybe on Edith? One was to check with Edith and Nestor, Earl Johnston's brother, who on reflection might be easier to find than Edith. The chance that Edith had been the real reason for the attack was remote, but I still felt stupid for not giving the possibility much weight. Her desk job with the intelligence agency seemed a remote source of Earl's attack and our fate, even considering my ignorance about her life.

I knocked on the door to her condo a couple times. No answer. I held my breath and hoped that I wouldn't be walking in on a setting for a stag film—years ago I had had a landlady walk in on my ex-wife and me as we were having a carnal heart-to-heart. Only the week before the attack, Edith had given me a key to her apartment, an indication that she was getting to trust me. Normally, she had visited me. I probably should have been more trusting of her as I stood at her door. The key worked when I tried it, and I walked in.

In the stale air quiet of Edith's apartment, her plants looked well-watered and well cared for, which indicated only that Edith had kept a lady from an apartment down the hall as a friend. The lady was Mrs. Kilmur, Lady Kilmur, if you will, as Edith referred to her. A widow, I'd met Lady Kilmur once in passing as Edith and I were heading out for food and diversion. Edith liked Mrs. Kilmur because she had been married to an English nobleman, or so he claimed, which meant English quality so far as Edith was concerned.

Now and then Edith would talk about Lady and the late Lord Kilmur, so I figured out a few things about him that I said nothing to Edith about. It didn't make any difference to Edith that Lord Kilmur had apparently supported his title with upper-class pretensions and hopes, shadowy, upper-middle-class finances, and a mysterious past. Between what Lord Kilmur bequeathed his Lady and the money that she had acquired on her own, Lady Kilmur had done well enough to afford a live-in maid. It was, in fact, the maid who looked in on Edith's apartment and watered the plants when Edith was away.

After a brief search through Edith's bedside address book, a private, dainty, leather covered volume, I found Lady Kilmur's phone number, which I dialed. Her maid, Agnes, answered. I asked Agnes if she knew what had happened to Edith. For my answer, I got Lady Kilmur herself on the phone, who invited me to come next door for a brief chat and a late snack. One last look through Edith's apartment revealed nothing.

To enter the Kilmur condo, you had to approach a beige door, plain except for a bronze-colored knocker, with "Kilmur" embossed on it in English gothic. A small, round, thick, sighting glass lens peered out just underneath the lettering. I knocked and watched the eye. It changed color as someone's shadow on the other side of the door darkened the lens. I stood for inspection.

"Mr. Chappell?" a young woman's voice called out, her voice muffled by the door.

"Yes."

"Lady Kilmur will be here to receive you in just a minute."

"I'll wait."

The peephole glass in the door went light and dark again. A few more moments passed. The glass went light. A few moments more and the door opened.

"Agnes?"

"Yes, Mr. Chappell. Will you follow me?"

Agnes and I entered a living room, larger than I thought the condo complex offered, almost as large as Edith's entire apartment. The room was just right for a soiree, or perhaps a reunion of gallant diplomats or other such souls who had served abroad in a hardship post in time of war. Judging from the décor of the room, the post abroad might have been in China before the Communists took over after the Second Great War. Or made in Taiwan. At any given gathering, someone probably played "A Kiss Is Just a Kiss" on the Steinway grand positioned in a dark part of the room, a Steinway decorated with a couple of long dragons intertwined on the underside of the opened lid. No one had lowered the lid after the party ended.

A rug with an intricate Chinese motif covered most of the floor. I was tempted to peer into two large Chinese vases—vases from the Ming Dynasty for all I knew, which was not much. They appeared fragile and expensive. I checked on the "management of the house" to see if the maid had overlooked emptying them of cigarette butts and ashes after the party, whenever it had been given. The vases proved to be filled with clean sand. What an elegant resting place for abandoned cigarettes and cigars. Lady Kilmur entered the room.

"Please forgive Agnes, Mr. Chappell, for saying that I would meet you at the door. She's still learning that I prefer to greet my guests in the salon."

"Yes, ma'am," Agnes said from the hall.

I was in for midnight surprises. For one thing, Lady Kilmur appeared to be in her late thirties; in fact, Edith had placed her as being in her fifties. During the one time that Lady Kilmur and I had met in passing, I could not estimate her age because she had worn a large, old-fashioned hat and veil that discouraged a close look at the real woman. Perhaps it was a disguise. Now, at the witching hour and in the middle of her Orientalia, Lady Kilmur was striking. Even as she came over to me, hand extended to be shaken or kissed, and even as I got a close look at her, scarcely a wrinkle could be seen, her skin smooth and Dresden white from a life indoors. I shook her hand even though I had the feeling that she preferred that I kiss the hand and the ring on it.

Lady Kilmur had invited me down for a snack, an informal gesture, only to surprise me with her high formality. Wearing my old sport coat and poplin slacks, I felt out of place and on the defensive, uncomfortable. How large would the candles be at the dinner table, I wondered in a moment of sarcasm. Without a preliminary gin and tonic, it took only a walk to the dining room to find out: 15-inch candles, their height equal to the diameter of a British naval gun. Four of those candles had been set. They proved sufficient to light the crested family crystal and silver set upon dark green placemats that rested on a dark, mahogany dining room table.

"Edith has told me so much about you," Lady Kilmur began as I held her chair for her. I wanted to be rude and tell her to cut the crap and tell me about Edith. She probably worshipped tact in the shrines she had built to manners in her home and would disdain any shortcuts I had in mind to this matter.

"I'm quite fond of her," she continued.

"So am I," I responded, as Agnes brought in two servings of eggs benedict. By jar or by egg, someone in the house had a quick hand for hollandaise sauce because it couldn't have been more than five, ten minutes at most since I had phoned and gotten the invitation. "Do you know where she is?"

"Approximately. Was that her apartment you were calling from?" she asked.

"Yes."

"Did you break into it?" she asked with a smile.

"With a key. Edith hasn't told you everything she knows about me."

"Edith trusts you."

"Yes. Have you seen Edith since yesterday? I've been trying to contact her, but she hasn't been answering her phone. She's left no indication of where she is."

"Isn't that her business?"

"We've known each other long enough to mix business."

"Normally I don't pry."

"But, as Edith told you when she phoned you from St. Michaels for the ride back to the Western Shore, someone attacked the two of us. I want to make sure she's all right."

"And you left her alone after that?"

"You put a high price on your hospitality, Lady Kilmur."

"Indeed, I do."

"Too high for me."

"Don't leave, Mr. Chappell. I was just checking, and I probably went too far. I'm very fond of Edith, as I've said. I gather that she's been in trouble, and I wanted a sense of your part in it before I told you where Edith is."

"Where is she?"

"I'm not sure I should tell you. After Agnes fetched her on Sunday for the ride back, Edith was quite disturbed. She talked of being afraid of something in her past… her husband, jealousy, and all that. She wondered if the person who attacked you had been hired by her husband… her ex-husband, rather… to get even with her. She left him. He's quite possessive. I know him, and he really is a nice man. I've wondered if you were nice. To put it another way, while Edith and I have been neighbors for only a couple of years, I have wondered if Edith's men are nice."

I didn't say anything, didn't rise to the bait.

"Edith also expressed concern about your safety," Lady Kilmur continued. "When she left last night, I think she returned to the restaurant on the Eastern Shore where you had a meal. Hattie's or the Half Way House? And she said something about going to a place called Tilghman's."

"Tilghman's Island."

"What a quaint name for the restaurant."

"Hattie doesn't think so. She prefers Half Way House."

"How amusing you are. I think I've eaten there, in fact."

"When was that?"

"A long time ago. What do you plan to do about Edith?"

"Did she say she would go anywhere else?"

"She planned to at least look at the home of the person who assaulted you and died, or perhaps see if his parents were available. The Johnstons."

"Do his parents live there?" I asked, trying to find out how much she knew about the problem.

"That's what the newspapers said in their stories about the murder. Didn't you read them?"

"It's been a while. You've got a keen memory."

"It's useful for finance."

"Did Edith tell you where she planned to spend the night?"

"The Easton Inn. You might phone her there now if you like. Feel free to use my phone. The phone number is on the card next to the phone. I stayed at the Inn two months ago."

"Business?"

"Yes," she replied. "There's a lot of money in Easton just waiting to be invested and reinvested wisely."

"Edith should have been back by now," I said. "There's not that much left to look for on Tilghman Neck."

"What did you find there? May I call you Robert?"

"Sure."

"Call me Melissa. Forget the Lady business. Did you find what you were after, Robert?" So, Melissa or Lady Kilmur, whatever, decided to try a little intimacy with me.

"It's too early to tell. There's a lot to sort out."

"What were you after?"

"Why the attack on Edith and me took place. There's always a chance of a repeat. I wanted to avoid that."

"You're big to be so cautious. It is late for Edith to return. As I suggested, why don't you try the Inn?"

While I dialed the Inn, I said to Lady Kilmur, "I'll bet you remember the Inn's phone number, as well as the numbers needed for investing and high finance."

"An accident of Nature."

The room clerk at the Inn told me that Edith had registered and that he would put me through to her room. The phone rang. No one answered.

I left Melissa's at about 11:00 p.m., which left me enough time to think about what else could be done before going to sleep. While I wanted to see Edith, I wasn't up for a three-hour drive to Easton, so I decided to return to Edith's apartment, make coffee, and figure out what was next. I slipped the key into the lock. Someone inside the apartment closed a door. I drew a breath and walked in.

Who should be there but Agnes, looking through Edith's address book? Lady Kilmur had sent her down during the eggs benedict to see if I "had missed anything, any note or such," at least this was Agnes' suspect explanation. At that hour, Melissa's curiosity about Edith was well over the top, however genuine the friendship.

Agnes cut quite a figure in the refined décor of Edith's apartment, for Agnes was tall, raw boned and big boned, and had quite a heft to her. She was probably clumsy around the house, prone to bumping into the family breakfront and placing the China in peril. The neat maid's uniform that Melissa had dressed her up in offered quite a contrast, dainty on big. The only other piece of daintiness appeared in a broach pinned at the throat of Agnes' blouse, a daintiness that disappeared on closer inspection. A whaling scene in scrimshaw decorated the broach. The scene depicted a whale rising from the ocean and throwing from his back toward heaven a boat filled with whalers, some tossed from the boat into the foaming sea. It was a desperate scene, drawn in fine, thin lines.

I asked Agnes if the broach were part of her uniform. No, it was hers alone, and had been in her family for years, an heirloom—her people had once been New England whalers. Agnes said she would have to return to the Kilmur apartment. But, while she was at it, she might as well dust the place. I pocketed a question to Agnes of what business did she have looking through Edith's phone book. After all, I knew little about how Edith, Melissa, and Agnes got along, even knowing that Edith and Melissa especially were close.

My waiting would have required too much effort, and I did not want to spend any more time around Agnes (and, through her, the weird and extended presence of Lady Melissa Kilmur), so I left a note telling Edith where I would be. I wished Agnes a fruitful effort. Rather than return to my apartment and face delay in getting to the business at hand on the morrow, I left for *Jupiter*. There, I would spend the rest of the night and be ready to approach Nestor first thing in the morning.

Almost did not make it. First, there was the battle against the temptation during the drive to pull off the road for a nap, because there was little to keep a person awake, virtually no traffic. At that hour of the night, the world around me consisted of my car and the view the headlights revealed. Other lights on and off the road could just as well have been the fireflies of another world. My passage to the Bay took place with little sense of time, and less of movement, beyond the mild vibrations of the car and hints of the side of the road passing by. My drive to Davidsonville took me along one of the lesser transportation spinal cords of the Northeast Corridor, helping to connect the part of the country that had won the Civil War with the part that hadn't. As such, I drove south on Ritchie Highway to Route 50. From there, I turned south again onto Route 2 and then to Route 214 before turning off onto Davidsonville Road.

I caught sight of what would become the second reason for my problems in getting to *Jupiter* when I turned off Route 50. In the darkness, I noticed a car following some distance behind me. At the time, I felt all alone. For lack of anything better to do, I kept on watching that car. The two of us traveled a few miles further, the car keeping its distance. I hung a quick right onto

Solomon's Road and made a quick left onto the narrow and winding Mill Swamp Road. I had just begun the long descent down that road when I realized that the car far behind me was now close to me, almost tailgating me. He had snuck up on me, I guess. It appeared to be a big car that bathed my car in a blaze of light.

In daylight, Mill Swamp Road would be a country pleasure to travel on, if you go for a road old enough for the traffic of two hundred years or more to have worn away the land under wheel, hoof, and foot, leaving high banks on the side of the road in several stretches. Woods and old farms live side by side in this part of the country, the woods also flanking the road and providing an arbor over it for much of its length. Daylight or moonlight would show hilly farmland beyond the trees, in some cases a few feet from the road, as if the farmland had worn away the forests.

It takes Mill Swamp Road a mile and a half, maybe two, downhill to get to the road to Galesville and *Jupiter*. The grade is steep enough for a car to coast much of the way, and even gain speed, despite the twists of the road. I was thinking of putting the gearshift into neutral in order to coast and save gas when the car following me bumped into me. No accident here; he meant business. Lucky for me, he made a mistake.

He should have made his move against me earlier, on the roads we had just left, for they were wide and straight enough for him to have started to pass me innocently enough and then, in a surprise move while passing, force me off the shoulder of the road into a ditch or fence post or even a ravine. There would have been no traffic and no witnesses, and no problems except for damage to his car. It would have been damage to his car, which in the deserted countryside would be anonymous and easy to repair later miles away in, say, Baltimore. His mistake meant that he was an amateur.

He tried again, bumping my car's rear bumper harder with his own. Only one thought came to me: drive as fast as the old car could take me and hope to lure him into a trap. The trap was tactical, drawing the driver behind me into taking a turn further down the road faster than an amateur caught by surprise could take, and counting on his ignorance of the road to do him in. Some luck was already with me. I was driving downhill, which allowed me to accelerate much faster than normal.

I moved out, and so did he. My car angled from one side of the road to the other as one turn led to another. His car lumbered behind.

I gained some distance from him but lost that distance as we came on a short straightaway. He hit me one last time, near the end of the straightaway, a few yards from where the gravel and the turn that I had pinned my hopes on began. My car almost let me down. The rear end skidded on the gravel and swung out to the side, causing the car to start traveling down the road sideways. I turned the steering wheel toward the direction we were headed. I hung on, prayed, hung on some more, kept the steering wheel turned, rode out the violent sways and lurches of the car, and eventually saw my car behave herself and straighten out.

The lights from the chase car disappeared from my mirror, a sign that he hadn't made the turn. I had been too busy to hear any telltale sound, and pulled over into a driveway to the left, turned out the lights, and stopped.

I waited, listened, and thought. First, the attack from Earl Johnston, and now an assault by a car. I could leave and wait for the next installment, under stars that might be less favorable. Or, I could go back and see what happened to the chase car. Doing so risked taking a bullet through my head, or perhaps a resumption of the chase, he in the car and me on foot. The prize that awaited me was survival, followed by the chance of finding a few more clues about what lay behind the violence against me.

Silence in the night. No sign of life behind me. I looked down the driveway into a clearing next to where a small light illuminated part of the Ralph Bunch community center. I turned off the ignition to my car. With my arm out the window in the cool of the night, I listened some more. Now, a few of the creatures of swamp and forest sounded in full voice, the late voices of fall. In slow motion, I got out of the car.

In the two or three minutes it took for me to walk back to the curve where the action had taken place, I still heard no man-made noise. In the distance, I saw a pair of car lights shining to the left, into the woods, where my pursuer's car was either plowing up the ground off the road or nuzzling the base of a tree. It was too far to tell for sure.

As I got closer, I could see steam rising from the crumpled

hood of the car. Except for the hissing of the steam, all continued to be silent. A figure in shadows slumped over the steering wheel. However, I could not get a close look at the driver before I had to run for cover. I heard a car coming down the road, its headlights revealing the road.

The new arrival barreled by, then skidded to a stop. From a thicket, I could make out several teenagers in the car, laughing and carrying on, apparently drunk out of their minds. Slowly they got out of their car, seemingly stiff from riding in it, and proceeded one by one toward the wreck, cautiously.

"Maybe we can rip something off the car," one of the said.

"There is a guy in there," another responded. "He looks hurt bad. We better get the cops."

"You get the cops," the first one answered. "I'm trying another joint and look the car over."

He drew a cigarette or marijuana nail from a pack, lit up, opened the car door next to the driver, and for a moment looked in towards him, and then opened the door to the back seat. There he found a bag, which he identified to the others as a doctor's bag, while the others stood around watching and telling him to hurry up. All this happened while the person in the car continued to slump over the steering wheel. He moaned, which panicked the teenagers, who piled back into their car and left.

Their departure gave me another chance to look over the car and driver. I'd never seen him before. As best I could tell, he was short and chunky, in his middle forties, gray hair for sideburns, and had blood on his forehead. The windshield was cracked where his head had hit it.

He stirred as I stood next to him. Instead of taking any more chances by seeking out his wallet, I wrote down his license number and left for my car. I was shaking. Just after I made it back to my car and had gotten in, a police car, siren on and lights rotating from its roof, sped past, going up Mill Swamp Road. After a bit, I started the engine and resumed my trip to *Jupiter*, just a few more miles down the road.

Hours more would have to pass before dawn would come. I made my way through the Rudd Yard, past a few large sail-boats, cradled out of the water for winter, their cloth wings tucked out of sight. I drove slowly past a large open-walled hanger with a corrugated roof that sheltered some of the gray heads of the yard: an old Matthews, Chris Crafts, and other powerboats. Powerboats were the smallest in number, but larg-est in size, of all the boats in the yard. Finally, I made it to *Jupiter*.

My headlights picked out Edith's car, parked near *Jupiter*'s slip. I locked my car, walked a few steps to the dock, and then to my boat, which I boarded. The screens to the main cabin had been inserted in place. I opened them to enter, only to see by the eerie lights cast by the yard into the boat a small revolver point-ed at me. Edith was standing in the cabin, holding a Ladies Home Journal special.

"Please put that gun away, Edith. I didn't know you carried

one of those."

"Self-defense, Robert," she said as she put it in her purse.

"I've been looking all over for you," I told her. "I went to your apartment to see if you were all right. I tried to phone you at the inn… Melissa said you'd gone there. Have you been in any trouble?"

"Not physically. But… I don't appreciate your sleeping with that chippy from the Bridge Restaurant."

She nailed me on that one.

"Why, Robert?" she continued.

"Look. I care enough about you to come looking for you." I had to sort out what I felt and what I had to say.

"And you came to your boat instead of to the Inn."

"I didn't know that you were there… Ah, yes, I slept with the waitress… well… because she was there. And I had a lapse."

"A 'lapse,' you call it!?"

"Yes. I don't know how you spend the hours and days when you are away from me. And, I couldn't get in touch with you. I didn't know you were at the Inn until your friend told me. I figured you had taken off again. I was lonely. As for the waitress, she invited herself in. She was looking for a free ride away from there and a meal ticket." My explanation felt hollow. How did Edith know?

"It's always the woman's fault, isn't it?" she ventured. "Well, at least you're honest. I never met a man who could resist temptation."

"The same goes for women, though this is probably not the

time to say so," I replied.

"Do you really think that of me?" Edith asked.

"I don't know enough about you to say for sure. But, it's probably true."

Edith remained quiet. Then, in the faint light in the cabin, she gave me a wan, sad smile and said, "You're probably right." I turned the lights on.

"Where'd you get the gun, and why do you carry it?" I asked.

"It's none of your business where I got it. And, if you can't figure out why I carry it, you're dumb."

"Who are you afraid of? Does the gun have anything to do with your job?"

"Hardly. My job, the kind of work I do. The office I work in has the personality of an insurance office. After last weekend's assault on the boat, you can hardly be surprised that I carry a gun. It's for personal protection. I need protection because the violence around us."

"So, you have no idea what caused the attack?" I asked.

"No."

"Your ex-husband?" I asked. "You mentioned his temper… I think he did try to run me off the road."

"He can be a problem, but he's not lethal. I just like a little extra protection. You never know when you can depend on a man for it."

"Your 'ex' wouldn't be a physician, would he?"

"He is."

"Small? Drives a big car?"

"Yes. Short and powerful. He could break your neck if you didn't watch out. Why do you ask?"

"Does he know about us?"

"Why are you asking me these questions?"

"Again, I think he's the fellow who tried to cut and compact me a few minutes ago by trying to run me off the road."

"How did you see him in the dark?"

"I got a partial look at him. He missed me and went off the road and cracked up his own car. The cops were coming to pick him up as I was leaving."

"Maybe it is Rudy. He is jealous. In fact, he still considers me his wife. His full name is Rudolpho Alexander, MD."

"I got his license plate number. I'll check it out in the morning. How come he waited until now before coming after me? You and I have known each other for months. Also, how did he know enough about me to track and follow me before his assault?"

"I have no idea," Edith replied. "I was going to say something to you about him… and, maybe he had something to do with the attack on the boat. Maybe the road incident. If so, it's news to me. But… what do you do when you've got one man being too concerned with me, and another not concerned enough?"

"If you're bringing up my bad form again, sleeping together is only part of the question. You've told me next to nothing about yourself. You disappear for days at a time without a word. How do I know you haven't cut out on me when you've had the chance?" I asked. Edith said nothing, so I continued, "You've got your privacy, but you've also only got half of me because of it. Sooner or later, you've got to share your privacy with anyone you want to owe you love. If I didn't care for you, I wouldn't have come looking for you."

"How do I know you've been looking?"

"Your friend, Lady Kilmur. She's the one who told me where you stayed on the Shore."

Edith remained silent.

"Anyway, I'm glad you're safe," I said.

She offered no reply. The two of us went to bed in silence, she to the fore berth, while I stayed in the main cabin on the quarter berth. Edith closed the door separating the forward and main cabins.

At one point during the remainder of the night, I awoke from a fitful sleep. I looked out through the main hatch at the other boats on the dock and at the dark creek and the woods beyond, and I grew uneasy. I'd been so tired going to bed that I had forgotten to close the hatch and put up the shutters.

None of the other boat or yard people were likely to be around at this hour, which meant no protection in numbers here. Anyone smarter than I was, anyone with more strength than I had, anyone with a knife or gun, could make short work of Edith and me. At that hour, it was easy to sympathize with ancient superstitions, such as those concerning devils and witches and other personifications of the worst that one person could do against another. There was more to such superstitions, namely that they serve as masks for symbols that populate the spiritual world of people. These are symbols with a vengeance. Almost anyone who ever lived, if the circumstances could be arranged, could stand in *Jupiter*'s cabin, look to the dark woods across the creek or up the road from which I had come, and wonder if some nameless force was preparing to attack, maim, and kill. A symbol without a face.

Round two of my negotiations with Edith started after a breakfast of canned fruit, canned milk on cereal, coffee, and monosyllables.

"How about clearing the air?" I began.

"What do you suggest?"

"We either split, or we forget the past and make up."

"As easy as that, Robert? ...I'm not going to forget what happened with you and your chippy waitress. But I'm not perfect. I would like to continue seeing you. Also," she continued with a trace of a smile, "I might want some moral credit from you sometime, in case I slip from the straight and narrow."

"Okay," I replied.

"While we're on the subject of the waitress," Edith continued, "you'd better watch out. You made a few enemies on that number."

"What do you mean?"

"I just missed you by a half an hour or so, Tuesday morning. You had just left to return to Galesville, apparently. In case you're interested, I found out about the waitress from a friend of hers, a boy who works at the gas station across the channel from the restaurant. I asked him if he had seen you and *Jupiter*. He asked me if I was a friend of yours. I said yes. He told me to give you the message that he and his friends plan to give you a proper goodbye. Then, he told me why—his friend and the waitress, the night she spent on the boat, and all that. I'd take it seriously, Robert."

"I am."

"Actually, the gas station attendant and his friends got in a motorboat as I was leaving; I think they did go looking for you."

"They missed me. My luck held. Did you find anything out about the Johnston family?"

"No. I was mostly worried about you. There was no way to reach you by phone, and I got too nervous to sit around and wait. So, I went looking for you."

"Is everything all right between you and Lady Kilmur?" I asked.

"I think so. Why do you ask?"

"She had me over at midnight last night for a snack, and she said she was concerned about you. She seemed nervous."

"She is possessive at times. But she's done a lot of favors for me, such as looking after the apartment. Or at least her maid does. Why do you think that something might be wrong?"

"She sent her maid to look through your belongings while I was eating at her place."

"Melissa was just being conscientious."

"At midnight? I'd call it being nosy with an odd sense of timing."

"Honestly, Robert, you are so suspicious. Um… incidentally, why were you at Melissa's at that hour?"

"I went to your place in search of you, Edith. As usual, I did not know where you were."

"You, Robert, are hardly Mr. Glued-In-One-Spot!"

"Edith, I phoned Melissa to see if she knew your whereabouts. That's all. She invited me for a late-evening snack and talk. More than that, I want to know what she is all about… and maybe commit a little burglary of the mind."

"Burglary of the mind? Melissa's mind? What are you talking about, Robert? What do you intend to do with your loot?"

"Understand what the hell is going on. Burglary is just a figure of speech."

"Robert, I don't blame you for being careful after the attack on *Jupiter*. There may be something in what you say, but you are taking your suspicions a bit far, don't you think, Robert? I mean, your inept attempt—as you put it—to burgle Melissa's mind? Melissa would not betray a trust."

"How long have you known Melissa?" I asked.

"Long enough to consider her and her late husband friends.

Robert… there's a lot you don't know about me, and a lot that I don't want to talk about now. Let's drop it, all right?"

In an attempt to calm Edith down, I told her that, as far as Rudy was concerned, Rudy was smarter and more determined than I had first given him credit for. Edith's response to me: "That's a start."

I addressed one last hunch to Edith. "Incidentally, the cops questioned you, didn't they?"

"Yes. There wasn't much that I could tell them. I didn't really see much of Mr. Johnston, you know."

"Did the police give any indication why Johnston had attacked the boat?"

"No. I remember vaguely that Rudy once introduced him to me, but I did not like him. Rudy caught my drift. Rudy generally does not mix work with home or friends."

I touched Edith's hair. We kissed. She said she really had to get back to the office since she had taken off the previous day to look for me—now that her furlough had ended. So, she left me to consider my unsatisfied love considering her request that I be patient. She promised to come to *Jupiter* after work, where we would sup together. I would tell her how my talk with Nestor Johnston had gone.

When I ambled in search of Nestor, who should I meet making his rounds in the yard but its manager, Tom Pemberton. He said the yard could repair or replace *Jupiter*'s bow pulpit any time I liked. I thanked him and gave him the okay for repairs. I asked if he had seen Nestor Johnston? No, but last night, the cops had picked Nestor up for questioning again. Pemberton said he wasn't sure why since the cops had just released him a short time before that.

A motorcycle, ridden by a young, lean fellow in a black leather jacket, came down the road. He stopped the cycle at one of the long, low, yard work sheds. Pemberton identified the rider as Nestor, said it was unusual for him to be late for work, and asked that I take it easy on Nestor because he was a nice kid who had gone through a lot since his brother's murder. As for Nestor, erect to his full height (a little shorter than me) after dismounting from his motorcycle, he said he couldn't talk because he had to work, but if I came back around 5:00 p.m., he would be glad to tell me whatever he could about his brother. Nestor explained that he would be happy to talk about his brother, with whom he was not close. With Nestor, work came first.

I phoned Detective Byrne to check in. He talked short with me, not liking my silence—I should have checked in with him, he explained, when I was in Tilghman. When I asked if he had a strong suspect for my assailant's murder, Byrne replied that he had told me all he could, given the silence he was supposed to keep about the status of ongoing investigations. I replied that as I was the victim of attempted murder, the case was damn well my business unless the department was short of things to do and wanted another corpse on their hands. Don't get paranoid, Byrne rejoined, any suspects in the Johnston death were still none of my business.

After leaving Byrne, I conducted a flyby along Mill Swamp Road, retracing my route of the night before through the autumn-splashed landscape. The offending car, a big Mercedes, lay in peace without an attendant or driver. I returned to the yard, phoned a friend at the *Herald* who was experienced in working with the Maryland Department of Motor Vehicles, and asked her to get the name of the owner of the Mercedes' license plate. Twenty minutes she called back. The car belonged to Rudolpho Alexander, MD, of 321 Foxcroft Lane, Bethesda, Maryland.

A phone call to the state police revealed that a Rudolpho Alexander had been admitted to the Anne Arundel General Hospital, in Annapolis, with injuries sustained from an automobile crash late last night.

Yet another phone call, this time to the hospital, disclosed that the good doctor Alexander was in room 2116 and, though sustaining a mild concussion and a broken arm, he was in fair condition. When I explained that I had to see the good doctor about an emergency in his family, I was told that in my case visiting hours would be relaxed. My last phone call was to Edith to see if she had any good advice for handling her ex. No answer.

At the hospital, I took the elevator to the second floor. When I got to the right ward, the halls were deserted. Of the patients I passed in their rooms, a few talked quietly with a visitor or two, some watched television, and a fair number just lay quietly in bed. A nurse came into view down the hall, then ducked into a room. At the far end of the hall, a woman began to yell. It sounded like Edith. The passion of the live voice contrasted with the snatches of tame agonies from a soap opera that emanated from one of the patients' rooms that I passed. As I drew near 2116, Edith's words came through loud and clear, "Mind you own damn business, I said!"

I'd never heard her swear before. A man's voice from the room was hard to understand, but he said something like, "Edith, you have no choice in this matter. You'd better tell your friend how I work. It will save you and him a lot of trouble. It may save him much more than that."

He spoke in a calm tone, as if providing medical advice to a patient about to undergo a major operation.

"More threats?" Edith answered. She broke out in tears. "Your God damn threats," she said with her voice breaking.

"There is nothing you can do about it," Dr. Rudy replied.

He gave me a choice. I could, like the good Marine I had once been, go over the top and have it out with him. Or I could be restrained and wait until a clear way to deal with him opened. Since he was indisposed and I was impatient, I chose to exploit his lack of mobility, and I walked in.

"This is private. Get out."

"You've got some medicine to take."

"You're not a physician… who are you?"

"You've followed me enough. You should know."

"Yes… Mr. Chappell. I should know."

Rudolpho Alexander, MD, came across as squat, mean, hard, and intense. He gave the impression of a man driven by an ambition to rule whatever was near him. If you had any doubts about his will, you'd better watch out. His face said it all, particularly his mouth: closed, it looked like a small staple on a pancake. For a moment, I wondered about Edith's taste in men. In husbands. "You have a vivid imagination, Mr. Chappell," Dr. Rudy continued. "You must love ghosts. Of course, you should always pay attention to your imagination."

"Heal thyself, Doctor."

"Ghosts can point out a moral. Ghosts can tell you when you've trespassed on what is not yours. Ghosts can warn you, as they did last night."

"What's your problem, Doc?"

"Your problem, Mr. Chappell!" He rose in bed.

"Your problem, Doctor, will soon be jail. There, you'll have a chance to rethink your professional reverence for life."

"Forget my profession. Look to your imaginings. Take your dream of last weekend and the attack against you on your boat. You almost got killed."

"The police will be interested in knowing how you know about that attack. The newspapers haven't published anything about it."

"The police would be bored. I learned about it from Melissa Kilmur and Edith. I had nothing to do with the attack. I just mention it as an object lesson to you and the care that you should have for your safety."

Edith kept quiet. She looked dazed by the proceedings.

"For a busted-up man whose medical license is in mortal danger, Doc, you look chipper. How long do you figure that's going to last?"

"Your threats about jail and my license mean nothing to me. I have plenty of money and don't need to practice. As for you, think about what I said. Pay attention to your dreams."

He had made clear his opinions. I had made mine. Time to leave. With Edith.

CHAPTER 7

The Soul of Good Humor

There was little point in trading more threats with Rudy. I needed time to think, to sort through what had happened. Had Rudy put Earl Johnston up to assaulting me and then paid him back with savage, medical surgery for his failure? One promising development had occurred: the threats against Edith and me seemed to come from recent hostilities and not from ancient grudges worked out from behind a veil of forgotten incidents in my life or hers. Not that recent causes couldn't be as dangerous as ancient ones. Recent incidents held more promise, being more vivid and easier to track to their origins.

"Why'd you marry him?" I asked Edith as we were leaving the hospital.

"I suppose I just wanted to get married, and Rudy came along at the right time. He's compelling, as you could see. He often gets his way when others don't want him to. I didn't know him well, and he swept me away, and the awful thing is that I still find him attractive. He's also, believe it or not, vulnerable."

"Attractive?"

"Yes. To me, anyway."

"I hesitate to ask why the two of you got divorced. He didn't leave you, did he?"

"No." Edith laughed. "He was, and is, a mix. Possessive as he is, he still didn't have any time for me because he was so absorbed in his work. However, at the same time, he cared for me—or wanted to own me, as you would put it—more than I wanted to own him. You don't have anything to worry about, Robert. The divorce is final. I'd hoped I could get my ex off my back and yours, without your getting into it. That doesn't seem possible now."

"I didn't realize that Rudy knew Lady Kilmur."

"Why do you call her Lady?"

"She's the only aristocrat I know, or wannabe aristocrat. And, I'm working off vibes from your attitudes you have about her."

"Yes, I like her a lot, especially her independence. She values herself. You don't seem to care much for her, Robert, even though she was kind enough to tell you where I was and to feed you a snack."

"She was as interested in getting information from me as I was in doing the same with her."

"Melissa and I go back a few years, Robert. When Rudy and I were married, we sometimes got together with Melissa and her husband when he was alive. In fact, Donald Kilmur—Lord Kilmur, if you like, or as he preferred—would give Rudy advice on money and even managed some of it. Rudy is quite wealthy, as he said in the hospital. Melissa is also an investment counselor and took over with Rudy after her husband died. She rather likes Dr. Rudy, I think. And, Rudy probably takes advantage of that when he can. He needs mothering. He maintains an independent friendship with her, independent of me."

"Do you think," I asked, "that Rudy uses Melissa to keep track of you?"

"Probably. I use her now and then to see what he's doing, when we're particularly on the outs. I see Rudy from time to time, for old time's sake."

"You don't think that she phoned Dr. Rudy after she fed me?"

"So he could follow you to Galesville?"

"Yes."

"Maybe. Maybe not. It's possible. I haven't seen that side of her. It's also possible that you're paranoid… though I don't blame you, considering recent events."

"Thank you. Do you have any suggestions for handling Rudy's attentions to us?" I asked.

"Rudy's behaving badly right now… I know… And Rudy might even be capable of hiring someone to assault you. But, to kill you? I doubt it. He takes his doctoring seriously, and that includes a reverence for life and curiosity about it. At times his curiosity may get the better of his reverence when researching the whys of anger in people."

"So, it was in the pursuit of research that he tried to run me off the road?"

"I know this situation looks funny, Robert. The only thing I can say is that this is the first time since I left him that he's gotten this upset. He's intense, usually. But, he's not a maniac. Rudy is, after all, a physician who takes his oaths to heal seriously."

"You're still coming down to *Jupiter* for supper?"

"Yes, indeed, Robert. I wouldn't miss it for the world."

At his office, Detective Byrne asked me to tell him again about Earl Johnston's assault on me. He let slip that the autopsy of Johnston's body had disclosed broken ribs as well as knife wounds. I explained that Earl had landed on his ribs when he jumped from *Jupiter* to his workboat, and his landing might have been one cause. Body blows I had delivered using the winch handle could have been another cause.

Byrne conceded that he and detective Saugers still had more information to go over, part of the large, general pile on their desks. So, he and Saugers still did not know much about the murder and my problems. Byrne did, however, agree to consider my complaint against Rudolpho Alexander, MD, Byrne agreed also to have a police lab expert look at my car and at Rudy's. A few minutes later, Byrne, the lab expert, and I made it to the police parking lot where both cars were parked and were looking at the damage to my car, especially at the busted rear bumper. I felt like a witch doctor in consultation with two other witch doctors over a sign, a mysterious sign, from the Gods. Yep, there had been recent damage to my car, the smile of fresh, cut steel showing through old paint. The damage, we all agreed, was a shame, considering—looking at the soul of my old Cadillac, beyond its dents and rust spots—that the car was something of a classic. Rudy's Mercedes likewise was hardly to be discarded. Afterward, Byrne said they would look over Dr. Rudy's car and get back to me if I could be found.

That consultation finished, I drove away surprised that detective Byrne had not raised a stink about my late report of the attack from Rudy and my abandonment of the accident "victim" at the scene of the accident. In fact, Byrne had expressed interest at the talk I had at the hospital with Dr. Rudy, and the possibility that Rudy might have killed Johnston. Even so, Byrne would not say anything about any suspicions he had about the Johnston murder. By his silence and discipline, he showed that he was a good cop, while I continued to be jiggled by circumstance and my speculations.

"I'm told that my brother gave you some grief, Mr. Chappell," Nestor Johnston said as we stood by one of the work sheds in the Rudd Yard.

"Well, he assaulted me in the middle of the night, and I didn't even know him. Do you have any idea why?"

"I don't think so. I never seen you in a family connection, but I seen you around the yard here. The only thing is, you look like you come from a family that my brother had trouble with."

"That's what I hear. I don't have family from around here. I never saw your brother before Friday night, when he first tried to pick a fight with me."

"Where was that?"

"The Clam Pier."

"I noticed him looking at you when you was in the yard and he had dropped by to see me. He could have followed you over there. He wouldn't be at a restaurant like that normally because it isn't his kind of place. Earl and me weren't close. I don't know why he came here to the yard Friday night, except to give me a hard time. But maybe something else was up."

Nestor thought for a moment, and then continued. "I mean something more than what he had been up to. He'd come to the Western Shore to get a little money. He'd already gotten a lot of money from this funny lady that he used to hang around with. She wanted him to do some kind of work for her. Anyway, Earl came down here to show off his money and rub it in. I don't have much money."

"Did Earl have a boat... a workboat?" I asked.

"No. Well, he sometimes borrowed one from the Whittier brothers. They're neighbors of my folks. Earl borrowed it without telling anyone, because that's the way Earl did things. The brothers let him get away with it."

"What was Earl doing for this lady?"

"I don't know, and I don't know who she was. He just said a couple words about it. The real money Earl was after was in Annapolis. He stole a car and robbed a grocery store there. Earl thought he'd stand a better chance of getting away if he went there using the boat as camouflage. He parked the car he took and left Annapolis by boat, and he got away with it. It's kind of a long way of doing it."

"Do the police know this, Nestor?"

"I told them after they picked me up and told me what happened to Earl."

"Did Earl get in fights very often? Did he ever kill anyone?"

"He loved to fight. He'd fight you if he didn't like your looks, and maybe he was crazy enough to kill someone. I always thought he killed his wife, though he never got convicted for it. Her brother got tried. I'm not sure about any conviction. Maybe my brother was crazy when he attacked you."

"I'd like to talk to your parents to see if they have any ideas about why Earl attacked me."

"They're hard to find these days. Their place burned down, and they're thinking about staying or moving away."

"I was on Tilghman Island when your parent's place was torched. I heard that people who did not like Earl were after his parents to pay them back now that Earl's dead."

"Why didn't you do anything about it?" Nestor asked.

"I didn't find out about it until afterward."

"Who told you, Mr. Chappell?"

"Somebody named Red Farrell. He works at the gas station, and I overheard him say something about it the next morning."

"He just works there. Was he in on what happened at my parents' place?"

"I'm not sure. A waitress at the Bridge Restaurant…"

"Laura Needham or Betsy Winters?"

"…Betsy. She…"

"Red's been after Betsy for years," Nestor broke in again. "She'd never have anything to do with him, except tease him and flaunt herself before him. Her boyfriend's a good friend of Reds. It's kind of strange."

Nestor had become excited, and his excitement, plus his changing the topic from the fire at his parents' place to Betsy Winters, made me wonder for a second if he was all there.

"Anyway," I continued, "Betsy said something about her boyfriend and Red and a few others getting together to see your parents. I don't know if they were the ones who burned the house."

"Did you tell the cops?"

"Yes," I replied. "In fact, I had mentioned it in passing to one of the cops while he, the police lab technician, and I were looking over my car. At the time they didn't express interest to follow up the information, so I let it be."

"The cops," Nestor said, "haven't said anything to me about it. Not that they would."

"Why should they? They're not going to take any risks on

behalf of someone else's revenge." One more possibility came to mind, so I asked Nestor, "Do you know anyone named Dr. Rudolpho Alexander?"

"The name sounds familiar."

"I thought Earl might have known him."

"Could be. I kept away from Earl as well as his friends."

"Was Earl once sent away to an insane asylum? Is that true?"

"Yes, sir. After his wife died or was murdered. He was let out a few months ago. That guy Alexander might have been taking care of him, but I'm not certain. I remember my parents saying something about him."

"I'd like to talk to them about Earl."

"I don't know. They're kind of... well... not your ordinary people. They're hard to find, especially after the fire and the cleanup. I've got to tell you, they're not anxious to meet new people these days, even if Earl caused you trouble. They're not likely to care much what Earl did to you."

"Look, Nestor, I'm not out for revenge or anything like it. All I want is some idea of why Earl was after me. Was he working for someone else who has it in for me? A grudge? This is hanging over my head. If someone else has it in for me, he or she will probably learn from your brother's failure."

"I'll ask them. If I see you, I'll tell you. If I don't, I'll leave a message on your boat. I can't promise anything. Okay?"

"Okay."

Opportunity is a pretty woman in despair. As Edith in her willowy fashion walked with grace toward *Jupiter*, I read bad news on her face. On the boat as I finished making a couple drinks for us, she told me that Rudy had phoned her during the afternoon to give her a hard time. Rudy asked Edith why it had taken the cops so long to question him about his accident and his intentions toward me. He asked her whether I had hesitated reporting the accident in the first place because I feared him? She winged it by telling Rudy that I was thinking of doing a variation on the Golden Rule: that I would do unto him as he was doing unto me, but I had stepped back and changed my mind.

"My feelings exactly," I told Edith.

Rudy also told her that his lawyer was working out arrangements for bail and that, in fact, he stood a good chance of having the charges dropped because of the long time it had taken me to report the accident and because I had left the scene of the accident. Rudy said he was even having his lawyer investigate the possibility of filing counter charges against me for having harassed him, having filed the complaint, however late, against him with the police.

Rudy was reaching too far for effect, I told Edith. A waste of money.

It was time to get away for the evening as best Edith and I could. Getting away meant giving up on the responsibility for cooking our own supper. It meant a drive to Annapolis to seek out a quiet restaurant on the waterfront. It also meant a quiet meal, if only because the Maryland legislature was out of session. Our luck fetched us the right kind of restaurant, which, at that hour of dusk, displayed more tables than customers, tables clothed by clean, white, tablecloths that cushioned settings of Japanese stainless steel and cafeteria glassware.

Edith and I spent the evening talking about everything but the causes and effects of our dilemma. It was only on the road back to Galesville that we got down to cases.

"What kind of doctor is Rudy?" I asked. "A psychiatrist?"

"He's a nerve specialist, Robert… and I'm not saying that to be funny. He was interested in being a psychiatrist at one time. He once said something about having once studied to be one, but something happened to him. He either failed a course, which I can't imagine, or he just gave it up, which is also unlike him."

"Has Rudy ever worked for a mental hospital?"

"Yes, I think so. It was a place on the Eastern Shore called Health-Wood. I didn't see him for the better part of two months during one period. He said he was trying out the job, though I really don't know what he was doing. We had a lot of trouble with each other then because he would get depressed. Maybe he committed himself to a hospital. Who knows? Do you think there's a connection between Rudy and Earl Johnston through the hospital? The policeman on the boat at St. Michaels said that Johnston had been committed, didn't he?"

"Yes. Johnston's brother, Nestor, said the same," I replied.

"That means finding out where Johnston was committed, and when," Edith continued.

"One lead would be the Johnston family, if they're available. If that doesn't work out, the police may have a record. Or I'll go to the library and work through their collection of telephone directories. One way or another, it'll work out."

When Edith and I returned to *Jupiter*, I found a note from Nestor saying that he wanted to see me again before taking me to his parents. Considering what they had gone through, that seemed reasonable enough. As Edith and I were leaving, I noticed that the damaged bow pulpit on *Jupiter* had been replaced, and I speculated that the Rudd Yard was more eager for business than I was to give it. At least the boat was fixed, and they had done a good job. So, they trusted me to pay them, which I would.

I checked my mailbox when Edith and I returned to my place in Pasadena. As we were entering my apartment, I realized that my safety could not be taken for granted. If Rudy wanted to ambush me again after he got well, my apartment, located in a neighborhood of declining maintenance and lingering pretensions, probably offered him more choice opportunities at me than a country road after midnight. However, for all the good my caution did me, nothing in my apartment was amiss.

The next stop was a return to Annapolis and Edith's. She had a much nicer place than mine, and I preferred it to mine. There we found a note from Melissa Kilmur inviting us to drop by for a snack and chat. Against my better judgment, I went along with Edith's wishes. She phoned Kilmur, found the invitation still holding, and the two of us went down the hall to the Kilmur place.

Agnes, the maid, had learned her lesson in introductions, for she led Edith and me to the living room where we were to be received, and received we were. Melissa Kilmur, in a light blue satin pants suit, sat in a chair near the piano. On a nearby couch sat a bandaged Dr. Rudolpho Alexander, smiling broadly, the soul of good humor.

"How'd you get out of the hospital?" Edith asked Dr. Rudy with astonishment.

"I walked out. I discharged myself. The bruises I got from the accident were misleading. It only looked as if I had broken bones. Turns out, just bruises. And some pain."

"That's all to the good," Edith replied.

"I'm sorry I shouted at you in the hospital, Edith. I'm supposed to be studying anger management in my patients. Looks like I'm in for a session of 'doctor, heal thyself.' I'm sorry."

"Apology accepted," Edith responded.

"As for you, Mr. Chappell," Dr. Rudy ventured.

"It's Robert."

"Okay, Robert, you've taught me a lesson. I've got to do better at looking beyond my own interests and needs. As you and Edith have probably guessed, it's hard for me to accept divorce. I'm also probably guilty of considering marriage at times as a question of property. In my world, I became a physician because of my success at self-discipline. At the same time, I have a poorly anchored instinct to help others so long that doing so does not get too personal. While I know medicine, I'm short of what you might call natural empathy, which can resist the calculation that can come from discipline. You can learn to ape the gestures of concern for others, which I employ now and then, but the divorce educated me in how far I must go to become a natural. You can't practice finesse and be clumsy."

"So," I interjected, "we're now buddies? Friends?" I wasn't entirely serious and looked for a way to bait Rudy.

"It's too early to tell," he replied. "Because of what has happened between us and because the two of us still seek the company of the same woman, there's no way of telling that I know of."

At this point, Melissa spoke: "At least we have a truce here."

CHAPTER 8

Experiment Therapy

The next morning, I got to thinking: yesterday evening had revealed possibilities for more anti-Chappell mischief. The possibilities began with the memory of having learned that Melissa and Rudy socialized and maybe even worked together, not that it was any surprise that, since the two of them lived in Edith's world, they should know each other. A social threesome. Eventually, I could not let my concern about Rudy and Melissa pass without comment.

Edith had shown no appreciation for my interrupting the scene in the hospital between her and Rudy, a scene which to me showed signs of starting to get nasty enough for Rudy to pose a threat to her. In the light of morning, she appeared to be unaware of that threat.

As a caution at the hospital, I had kept in mind a story that a veteran newspaperman told me when I was starting out as a journalist. When my friend was about to begin his career, he prepared for maturity and true life by going to bars and developing a taste for what they served. A fellow patron and a woman, with whom the patron was with, maybe his wife, began to get physical and fight, and she was getting the worst of it. In the name of chivalry, my friend stepped into the fight, only to have the woman turn and assault him in defense of her husband or escort, whatever he was.

Well, Rudy and Edith had once been married. Who knew, beyond appearances, what loyalty between them endured? I didn't know. In fact, what was Edith doing with Dr. Rudy at the hospital in the first place?

Before I could ask, Edith broke the silence between us, saying, "Thank you, Robert, for remaining civil and patient with Rudy and Melissa. There may be something to your lack of trust toward them, but I don't think so. Melissa did her best this evening to patch things up. Judging from appearances, Rudy has backed off. He may even be coming to terms with you."

"So far as you know? What don't you know?" I responded. "Isn't that hedging your bets, Edith? Rudy, more controlled? To me he remains a quick change from agreeable to hate, according to the moment. For all I know he also has a key to your apartment—who knows what mischief he might commit in the kind of rage he showed you in the hospital."

"Robert! First of all, you're the one who Rudy has a problem with, and I don't see what that has to do with my condo or who has a key to it. As for keys to my apartment, it's enough to know that I gave you one. I'm not accountable to you. In fact, you are crowding me! Back off! Your paranoia, apart from its justification, is starting to burden your charm. Yes, Rudy's pursuit of you and the accident that followed does not look good for the two of you. Once again, there's a lot you don't know... But I seriously doubt that I have anything to worry about so far as he's concerned. There's a lot you don't know about me, and a lot that I don't want to talk about now. Let's drop it, all right? Trust me."

So, we let the matter drop. Her anger at me receded, and the two of us managed to find the same bed to sleep in even though I had to brave another of Edith's looks of resignation before I checked the locks on the front door and the windows. I left the light on in the front room while holding the remote fear that anyone interested in reviewing the apartment during the night would think that one of its occupants couldn't sleep.

"You did right to phone before coming, Mr. Chappell," Detective Byrne said to me as I walked up to his desk. Relations between Edith and me restored to near normal, I was up for another try at finding out what mischief Dr. Rudy Alexander had been up to, despite the risk of Edith's disapproval. "I was about to leave," Byrne continued, smiling slightly. "You said you wanted to discuss the Johnston case some more."

"Yes."

"Any more attempts on your life?"

"No. I'd like to get ahead of any future attempts by talking to you."

"Do you want police protection?"

"Maybe. See what you think after we talk."

I told Byrne I'd followed up on the possibility that Rudy had underwritten the attack on Edith and me while we were on *Jupiter*, and asked Byrne to check the Health-Wood asylum to see if Rudy had worked there when Earl Johnston had been committed there. Posing as an old friend of Rudy's, I had already phoned Health-Wood before driving to Annapolis. How could I get in touch with him, I asked? I'd lost his phone number. The telephone operator at Health-Wood had been evasive, saying that, well, maybe someone by that name had worked there a while back, and maybe not. She could not give me an official answer unless I was on official business. Company policy. So, before coming to see Byrne, I had borrowed a photograph of Rudy—one that Edith had squirreled away—and loaned it to Byrne, who said he would check out my lead.

While I was at it, I mentioned my attempt to see the Johnston parents. He expressed interest in that too and said he had been looking for them since the fire at their place. What was behind that, he mused? Byrne said he kept in mind Earl's track record with the police. The Johnstons, as he saw it, qualified in part as suspicious of the law and partly as the original hard-luck family. I returned to Rudy again, about Rudy's attempt at reconciliation during the snack and chat, and about my fears that Rudy was trying a change of pace to set Edith and me up for another attack.

"Why Edith?" Byrne asked.

"He doesn't like her running off with me... even though he's divorced from her."

"And his motive in all this? Bad loser?"

"That's part of it. He hasn't put down the torch he carries for his ex-wife. But his ex—my girlfriend—are part of it because my girlfriend retains ties to him."

"Messy."

"Yep."

While talking to Byrne, I wondered if I weren't in an extra-large confessional, telling my troubles to a priest of the state who stopped short of offering me a Hail Mary. He seemed understanding in a cool, distant way, cynical though patient. As a civil priest, saving souls meant saving lives now and then, even though much of his work consisted of writing reports and, in his part of the world, keeping a tally of injuries sustained by the public, his flock. A quiet evangelist for law and order. Byrne seemed to value his work as serious. More than routine. One case after another. No burnout.

Rising to leave, I told him, "If you put a tail on me, you will find out where the Johnston family is... right?"

"Mr. Chappell, as far as the danger you fear, it's unlikely we would go to the expense and manpower of protection or even putting a tail on you."

"Why don't you give me information in exchange for the information I'll be leading you to?"

"Because I'm working for the law, by the book, and the

book says no."

"I'm working to stay alive."

"What do you have in mind, Mr. Chappell?"

"Going to Health-Wood with you."

"What would it accomplish, Mr. Chappell? Besides, don't you have to get to work?"

"I'm on vacation. Health-Wood would give me more of a feel for the situation."

"Some vacation. Mr. Chappell, in this situation, I'm the pro. Even though you have experience as a journalist, you're the amateur, and amateurs get hurt. I can't carry civilians along on police business. You, as a reporter, should know that. You've had trouble, and you don't want more, and I'll do my best for you. If I find out anything at Health-Wood that would help you protect yourself, I'll let you know. You going to see the Johnstons now?"

"I'll have to wait until their other son, Nestor, gets off work from the yard where I keep my boat. Ask your man to meet me at the Rudd Yard in Galesville. About 4:00 p.m., at my boat, *Jupiter*, slip 709."

"If anyone tailed you, it would probably be me or Detective Saugers, who's also working on this case. I don't think we'll be able to, though. Whatever happens, though, call me after you talk to the Johnstons. Okay?"

~

"You're lucky, Mr. Chappell," Nestor said.

"How so?"

"My folks didn't want to talk to you. At first, they wanted me to tell you that they didn't know anything."

"Why'd they change their mind?"

"They want to ask you a few questions."

"About what?"

"Don't know for sure. Something to do with money that Earl had been getting. They want to see who Earl was getting it from. My folks think that, with your poking and prying, you might have some answers for them."

"Do your folks want the money, or what?"

"Guess so. They'll have to tell you."

Nestor and I were in my car, driving back to Tilghman's Neck and Earl Johnston country. I had to make the trip with Nestor if I were going to talk to his parents. Nestor had surprised me just after lunch, when I showed up at the Rudd Yard, saying that if we were going to see his parents, we'd have to do it then. It would be the only chance I had.

I wasn't happy going solo. It would have been nice to play it safe and be more certain about what support, if any, the police could provide me. My going solo meant traveling with a stranger, with the brother of the man who had assaulted me, going to a dangerous place, taking another chance on "local justice." Once again, I was entering a region where police and lawyers intrude only to pick up whatever remains from the serving of that justice.

We turned onto the road that led to the Johnston place. In just a couple of days, it had become a see-through fortress: a tall, chain link fence had been built around the property, and a chain link gate barred further access to the road. Down the driveway into their place, I could see that ashes and other wreckage from the house had been bulldozed to one side, where it lay in a pile. On the site of where the house had stood raw clay that could be seen among the weeds and patchy lawn that made up the rest of the yard. Next to the clay sat a new house trailer, an indication that the Johnstons planned to stay and build again, having cleared the site, and put in temporary quarters as preparation for doing so. No car was in sight, however, which suggested that no one was at home to receive callers.

"Somebody has money," I said while Nestor and I looked over the situation.

He smiled and said, "It sure ain't me. You got a boat, though. You got money."

"A little, anyway. What does your father do, Nestor?"

"He's retired military, Mr. Chappell. He was a warrant officer. After he served in 'Nam, he said he never wanted to serve in the Army again, so he retired and got out."

"He must have done all right as a warrant officer to afford that fence."

"Yep. He made some money in Viet Nam. There's never enough of it, I guess. You better not talk about it with Pappy unless he asks you, which I expect he will. He likes to talk about where he'll get more money, not where he's gotten what he has."

"You all come from the Carolinas, don't you?"

"Florida, originally."

"Why'd you move north? Most people move south if they get the chance."

"It's all the same. Don't matter where you live—to Pappy anyway."

"Nobody's home, I guess."

"Can't be sure," Nestor replied. "Pappy may have this place rigged. He says he put in a few land mines yesterday to keep trespassers away. He's got a strange sense of humor, if that is what it is. I don't know whether he did so, or if he fixed them to blow if we walked or drove on them."

"Could be. Who's to know unless they're trespassing?"

Nestor got out of the car to push a button, part of a gray, metal box with a speaker on it. The box was mounted on one of the gate posts. Nothing happened. He tried again. When he got no response the second time, he returned to my car and got back in.

"Looks like nobody's home. If they was, the gate would open up. We'd drive in, and we'd be okay even though Pappy happened to set up the mine that way."

"You mean he buried mines in the road to his house?"

"I don't really know. If he did, he did a good job. Can't tell where, can you?"

"I guess not."

"Let's get something to eat. My parents may be at the Half Way House."

"Weren't they asked to leave from there a few weeks ago?"

"You checked us out? Mr. Chappell."

"I had to."

"The people at the restaurant are nice. They let my parents back in after the fire. They helped us out even though they didn't have to. 'Course, they are close by."

"Nestor, I'm not popular there. I'd be uneasy about going back."

"Don't be afraid about the restaurant, Mr. Chappell. I can see that you can take care of yourself. Besides, if you want to see my parents, you'd better take the chance now. Like I say, they're changeable, both of them."

Like a great, blue heron poised in a small pond, waiting for a minnow to swim close enough for supper, Mrs. Lucinda Hughes stood at the other end of the dining room, ready to receive the next customer. She walked slowly toward Nestor and me. After one of her eyes twitched when taking a second look at me, or so I thought, she started to show the two of us to where Nestor's parents were eating.

On the way there, however, I excused myself to make a pay phone call, the phone being in the next room. I called Edith at her apartment to tell her where I was and to ask her not to wait on me for supper. Detective Byrne was out, so I left messages for him at his office and at Health-Wood, again telling him where I was and, as best I could, stating what my intentions were, namely, to follow the Johnstons until I'd gotten what information I could out of them. On my way back to the dining room, I met Mrs. Hughes.

"Why are you back, Mr. Chappell?" she asked without a smile.

"To talk to the Johnston family."

"To persevere, when it comes to your own interests. I'll say that for you."

"What do you mean, Mrs. Hughes?"

"Well, you surely were not looking after Betsy's interests."

I probably should have told Mrs. Hughes to mind her own business, but instead, I asked, "Why do you say that?" I wanted to learn if she knew something that I should know.

"I've lost a very good waitress, Mr. Chappell. Betsy left. When she went, she had a black eye and a lot of bruises. Her boyfriend worked her over. If you had not taken advantage of her, she would have been spared that. To make matters worse, your wife, or whoever she is, was in here asking for you."

"When was that?"

"The day after the Johnston place burned. Mr. Chappell, what exactly are you up to?"

"I'm sorry to hear about Betsy."

"Sorry is a word used by someone who knows how to do

better but isn't up to it. You could almost be arrested for statutory rape, you know. She just turned eighteen a few months ago. You're too old for her, and you know it!"

"Where is Betsy, Mrs. Hughes?"

"I haven't the faintest idea. She simply has left."

"Mrs. Hughes, Betsy told me she was planning to leave anyway. In fact, she wanted to leave by moving in with me."

"So, you gave her an audition? How nice of you. Or, did she force herself on you?"

"No more, I expect, than she forced herself on the man she was living with."

"She could have had a marriage with him… eventually."

"Maybe, but not happiness or dignity. He beat her up a lot, didn't he?"

"Yes, but…"

"What kind of friend are you to wish that on her? You make Betsy out to be an innocent."

"Mr. Chappell…" Mrs. Hughes was getting red in the face and was about to burst into tears, "You could have helped her out, and you didn't. You knew better. She didn't. You are an intruder. And… you are trifling with one of our people. We are conservative here. Most of us go to church. After we settle down from being young, we work hard and live quiet, good lives. That's what Betsy's future was before you showed up, before you brought your slick ways here. Yes, Betsy had a rough life, but it was leading to a good life because her boyfriend loves her, and love makes it all turn out right. But, you wouldn't know that, I expect… One thing is for sure. You can count on getting yours from Betsy's boyfriend."

She gave a big sigh and, without further comment, turned away to look through a pile of receipts.

From where the Johnston family sat, you could see much of Knapp's Narrows by looking out a window next to the Johnston table. You could see the bridge and, on the other side of the canal, the gas station, which appeared to be deserted. At the Johnston table, Mrs. Johnston had the build, complexion, and the appearance of someone who had fought for many a lost cause in a bar room and had put on weight to make up for her disappointments. Pappy Johnston, on the other hand, was the fellow, all right, who had come busting out onto his back porch with a shotgun, and who had winged me. You could also see that Nestor's looks favored his father. Pappy remained combat ready, being fit, alert, and not missing a trick. If anything, Pappy carried less weight than Nestor, all of Pappy's weight going to bone and muscle. On top of his impressive torso rested the head of a man aging rapidly: hair mostly gray, well-wrinkled skin sickled over with a porcelain cast. Pappy's knotted and scrawny neck showed his age the most.

"You seen me before?" Pappy asked me through a half smile as I pulled my chair up to the table.

"Nope. Why do you ask?"

"Thought I seen you before."

"Where?"

"Riding around this country in a borrowed car, looking for trouble," he replied.

"Nestor tells me you're looking for money?" I asked, hoping to draw some of the sting from Pappy and to avoid having him increase his anger by feeding on it.

"You're not trying to change the subject, Chappell, are you? It is Chappell?"

"Yes, on both counts. I'm trying to find out what we can trade, not how we can fight. You can do that any time."

"You can bet your ass on that, Chappell. And, I can beat the piss out of you any time," he said, rising from his chair.

I rose at the same time and said, "You're welcome to try, old man. Let's go outside and see what you can do. You can forget about what I know concerning your son's death... or his money."

"Screw!" Pappy said with contempt. Nestor had gotten up too, and it looked as if he wanted in on the action to help his old man out. So be it.

At this point, Mrs. Hughes dropped by our table to see if we were happy and if the service was satisfactory. She also wanted to find out if we were thinking of leaving before Nestor and I had been served—Pappy and Mae had already eaten. Pappy assured her that everything was all right. We were just standing to get the wrinkles out of our trousers, and he wanted to see how big a man I was. Nestor and I went ahead and ordered our meals.

"You ever in the Marines?" Pappy asked me.

"You want to talk or fight?"

"Thought you was in the Marines. Is it true that the Marines are big on glory, small on sticking it out?"

"Why was Earl after me?"

"Beats me," Pappy said. "What do you think, Mae?"

"Mr. Chappell, neither of us really knows what our son was doing or why he attacked you, if he did." She spoke quietly and eloquently, belying her appearance. "The police came to us after Earl's body was found by a neighbor. The police said that you had filed a complaint that Earl had attacked you in your boat, the night that he was killed. Is that right?"

"Yes."

"Did you kill him and drop his body off?" Mae Johnston asked. "The police seem to think that you didn't. They have asked questions about whether you and Earl knew each other, and Pappy and I had to say that we did not know."

"I didn't know him. The only contact that I had with him began last Friday night in Galesville on the Western Shore when he tried to start a fight with me. I'd never seen him or met him. On Saturday night at a restaurant in St. Michaels, he tried again. Then, a couple hours after dark on my boat, he attacked me outright. That is all I know about him. That's why this whole situation is so screwy."

"Do you have any other interest in this?" Mae continued.

"Hell, Mae… he's not going to tell you or me," Pappy broke in.

"What are you two talking about?"

"Mr. Chappell," Mae continued, "you look like you once had money and now could use some more."

"Mae, he's already getting paid. What he needs is more money from us than he's getting from them. What's your price, Chappell?" Pappy asked.

The waitress came with the food, broiled blue for Nestor, broiled scallops for me.

"My price is information. Why did your son try to kill me? While you're at it, you might tell me who 'them' are."

Pappy sat back in his chair, squinted at his wife, and observed, "We got a real joker here, Mae," and turned on me, saying: "You show up out of nowhere. You look innocent and ask why my dead son tried to assault you… or kill you. You poke around here, asking about me and my family as if you was a newspaper reporter or something. What did you do to Earl to rile him? You're traveling under false pretenses for what should be out in the open. Why? What do you have to hide, unless it's that you're working for someone else?"

"I am a small-time reporter. I've been working at one newspaper after another for a decade. Now I work for the *Anne Arundel Herald*. Sometimes I free-lance for the *Washington Post* and other papers, and if you'd checked me out, you'd know that."

Nobody said anything for a while. Pappy picked up his fork and tried to take one of my scallops with it. He just would not back off. I took my fork and jabbed his hand with it. He didn't lose any blood; he did withdraw his hand. I asked him: "Why don't you check me out? I don't know any of your friends or your enemies. I don't know anybody over here on Tilghman. And, if you think that someone, anyone, is paying me to spy on you, you're dead wrong."

I turned to Nestor and continued, "You said your parents wanted to know about Earl. What do I have to do with Vietnam graft?"

Nestor looked at his food while his mother responded:

"Mr. Chappell, we don't know much about you. We have enemies from my husband's years in the Army. He was in certain special forces. He had some unusual assignments. We are afraid that Earl may have been killed by those enemies as a sign to Pappy and me of what's to come for us. We don't know what or who you represent. There's a good chance that Earl was checking up on one of our enemies when he was killed—it's a possibility. This is a private matter. That's why we have not mentioned it to the police."

Pappy stiffened at her last statement.

"You didn't want to burden the police with idle speculation?" I asked.

"Yes, that's it, partly."

"Of course, Mrs. Johnston," I continued, "there's always the problem that the Feds from Treasury might raise about your money. And, there's Customs."

Nestor and I had eaten quickly. We finished in silence. No dessert. I could see across the canal, at the gas station, Red was gassing up a car.

"There's not much more to say," Mae said.

"Why are you telling me what you have told me? Why are you even talking to me?" I asked.

"We can make a deal," Mae continued.

"You've got the wrong man. I'm not who you think I am. There's only one reason why I'm here: to find out why Earl tried to kill me. I want to do what I can to prevent another attack on me by someone else. In fact, I don't know if there is anyone else, except for one person. Could Earl have attacked me out of a case of mistaken identity? People have been telling me that I look like a Markus, even though I have never met one."

"You do," Mae said.

"Could the Markuses be agents for your enemies?" I asked, just for the sport of promoting local paranoia.

"Wouldn't put it past them," Pappy replied.

"They're local people, or were," Mae said. "You don't want to make enemies needlessly. They don't know anyone in the Army that you knew, Pappy."

Pappy said nothing.

"Mrs. Johnston…" I began.

"Mae. Please call me Mae."

"Okay. Did you ever meet the doctor who was treating Earl when he was in the asylum?"

"Dr. Alexander?"

"Yes."

"He was over to the house a few times. A little while ago. Dr. Rudolpho was peculiar but nice."

"Earl was under his care?" I asked.

"Yes," she replied.

"Why did Dr. Alexander visit you?"

"He wanted to see what the home environment had been for Earl when he was growing up. Also, Dr. Rudolpho got to like Earl as he was treating him. The doctor used to pay Earl expenses for taking part in a psychological experiment. I think the government paid for the experiment. Dr. Rudolpho said the experiment was designed to keep people like Earl from getting carried away by their anger."

"What was the experiment?" I asked.

"Had something to do with a technique the doctor called 'saturation therapy,'" Mae responded.

"What kind of therapy is that?" I continued.

"Means getting too much of a good thing," Pappy ventured.

"Pappy!" Mae reacted. "Dr. Rudolpho explained it by saying that he was trying to cure Earl's violence by giving him too much of it."

"Would Alexander have Earl beat up other patients—is that how his treatment or experiment worked?"

"I don't know about that part, Robert," Mae said. "I do know that he made Earl watch a good many violent movies. Also, Earl had to do a lot of exercise, the kind that let him work out his feelings against something. Handball, I think. Earl would have to hit and hit that ball for hours on end at the hospital."

"Did the experiments on Earl work?" I asked.

"Can a hog get too many slops?" Pappy ventured.

I looked at Mae, who said with a sigh, "It's hard to tell. Earl seemed calmed down after one of his sessions with the handball and the movies. There may have been other treatments, maybe some beating. It seemed to me that the treatments only whetted his appetite after his satisfactions wore off."

"Do you think Earl was receiving the right treatment?" I asked.

"I don't know," Mae said.

Pappy laughed, "It must have been right for something."

"Did Earl live at home with you, or did he have his own place?" I asked.

"Did both," Mae responded. "He had a shack by the river near Greensborough. Know where that is?"

"It's near the Delaware line. The upper part of the Choptank River."

"Yes," Mae said. "We're going up there in the next day or so to clean out Earl's stuff. We're going to sell the place. We bought it as a wedding present for Earl and his wife."

"Could I take a look at it?" I asked. "I might find something to help me."

Pappy and Mae glanced at each other. He shrugged his shoulders.

"Guess it would be all right," Mae said. "We don't know what shape the place is in. Probably hasn't been cleaned in some time. It's probably a mess."

"Is there any chance of going tomorrow morning?" I asked. "If there was any unusual connection between Earl and

Dr. Alexander, I'd like to find out about it as soon as possible."

"Unusual?" Nestor said.

"If Alexander was trying to use Earl to get at me. He's the ex-husband of my girlfriend."

"We'll go to Earl's place tomorrow," Pappy said. "Be at our place at 10:00 hours."

Time to return to Annapolis.

CHAPTER 9

Rudy or Not?

However, instead of Annapolis, I returned to Galesville and *Jupiter*, the better to prepare for tomorrow. "Eight-thirty, tomorrow morning it is, by my boat. That should give us enough time," I said to Nestor when I dropped him off at the Rudd Yard. Then I went to check on *Jupiter*.

Looking at her, floating on the quiet water, the evening light in decline, I realized that my sense of danger had slackened since my talk with the Johnstons and the ride back with Nestor. I was getting careless. That carelessness spoke poorly for a member of the species, the species to which I belonged, that congratulated itself, by word and song, on its ability to survive and persevere. The pleasure of feeling the warmth of an October sun and of seeing the reds, scarlets, oranges, and other colors of autumnal death in the woods and fields—before the cold black and white soon to come—had taken me from the cares of the flesh to the dreams of the spirit. It was a possibility that alerted me again to my danger: the possibility that, as natural and innocent as *Jupiter* looked at her slip, she could be carrying a death trap. She would be an ideal place for one.

Before boarding *Jupiter*, I looked her over with care. The new padlock and its setting to the main hatch remained intact, apparently untouched since I had left the boat. The forward hatch, locked from the inside of *Jupiter*, likewise appeared all right, and, after I had boarded the boat and pulled on that hatch, it remained shut as it should.

Back to *Jupiter's* cockpit, I unlocked the main hatch and opened it a hair. I peered into the gloom and saw no strings attached to the hatch and no shotgun pointed my way with another string attached to its trigger. There were no other surprises in sight either, so I carefully opened the main hatch the rest of the way. So far, so good. To make sure that *Jupiter* was safe, I searched her from keel to coach roof and found her safe, and finding her okay and having nothing else to do at the moment, I decided to relax from a wearing day by futzing around. I had dismantled part of the head to check on a noisy part when I heard my name being called from the dock.

"You there, Mr. Chappell?"

It was Detective Byrne.

"Come aboard," I replied.

Jupiter listed slightly under the good detective's weight.

"Don't walk around much, if you don't mind," I continued. "You'll scuff up my boat with the leather soles on your shoes."

"I know. Sorry about that," Byrne replied. He sat in the cockpit, peered into the cabin, and then looked at me. It was becoming Friday night. I was overdue for meeting Edith and supping with her.

"Nice boat you've got here, Mr. Chappell. I was in the neighborhood and thought I'd drop by. I live near here."

I gestured him to come down into the cabin, which he did.

"Like a beer?"

"Don't mind if I do. I'm off duty." Byrne did not seem the type of cop or detective to go on vacation, even for an hour. He also came across as more social, more outgoing and friendly, than most of the police I had known, careful to avoid discussing their work except with fellow officers whom they trust.

I asked, "You work overtime? Is there that much crime?"

Byrne laughed. "Yes. I'm on my way back to the barracks. Had to take care of a problem at home. You find the Johnstons?"

"Yes. They're public again, and I didn't find any trouble. They're back at their home site, on Tilghman Island. They've rented a trailer and had a big chain-link fence put up in record time for protection. They've even booby-trapped the yard, I think."

"With what?" Byrne asked.

"Land mines. That's what Nestor, their son, says. I don't know if he was pulling my leg. Pappy Johnston is an old Army man, retired, I guess. Nestor showed me the way to them over there. I could have found it myself. Nestor probably went along for the ride, and maybe he wanted to protect his parents in case I started anything. I don't know what the secrecy is all about, except that the Johnstons seemed to be hard and suspicious people."

"With their son dead, they have reason to be."

"Yes, but it's more than that. They came into some money in Vietnam, and I would be surprised if it were legal. But I can't prove anything. What did you find out at the asylum about Rudy?"

"Alexander and the deceased knew each other at Health-Wood. You were right. Johnston was a patient of the doctor's."

"Did you find out anything about the way that Dr. Rudy was treating or experimenting with Johnston? Anything unusual or weird?"

"In an asylum, Mr. Chappell, you're bound to find unusual treatments for unusual people."

"This would be extreme."

"Mr. Chappell, insanity is extreme. What are you driving at?"

"It could be that the attack on my girlfriend and me grew out of the treatments that Dr. Alexander put Earl Johnston through."

"Maybe. You should let the law take care of this. I can look into putting you under protective custody if you want."

"That won't work. How long would I have to be under

wraps? Until you figure what the score is with Alexander?"

"I can't say. A few days, maybe. You know… Dr. Alexander's free. Not much to hold him on. I should have told you that before. We'll clean up the whole mess soon."

"You mean, find the connection between Earl's death and the assault on me?"

"Earl's death… and your problem. Mr. Chappell, you think that you are big enough to take care of yourself under normal circumstances. Do I have to remind you? These are not normal circumstances. Take my advice: You can get hurt. Dr. Alexander can get hurt. There's been enough bloodshed without your adding to it. I've got to be truthful with you. We haven't had much luck in finding anything on Dr. Alexander that would show he's trying to kill you. For one thing, he has no criminal record. And we've been unable to turn up any report or evidence that he's capable of being a killer, directly or indirectly."

"You tell me to be careful, Mr. Byrne, but you're close with the information I need to protect myself."

"I appreciate the information you gave me. I just gave you some background on him. You going out and shooting Alexander, regardless of what I've got to say? Is that your solution?"

"Not hardly. I'm for self-protection, not revenge. You know a whole lot more about this case than I do. I need all the information I can get to protect myself!"

"Mr. Chappell, you think like an amateur. You don't know who's after you. Maybe nobody. You just have suspicions, the same as me, and my suspicions have about the same authority now as gossip. Another thing, the police department can't even rule you out completely as a suspect in the death of Earl Johnston."

"Does the department want to put me in protective custody to protect a suspect?"

"No. The law should act in your place, on your behalf. Get out of the way and let the law do its work, Mr. Chappell. It's better all around."

"By the time the law gets around to protecting my interests, I may not be alive to enjoy them, the way this case is going. If there was much chance of your figuring out what Alexander is up to, I'd go into exile as you suggest for a couple of days. But there's not much of a chance."

"Why?"

"Looking into what Dr. Rudy wants is just one of many things that you and the rest of the police have to do. How many are there of you working on the case? "

"Mr. Chappell…"

"How many are there of you on the case? A week's gone by, and there have been no arrests in the Johnston death. You don't have the time for Dr. Rudy that I do. I'm better off trying to find out what he's up to while he hasn't had a chance to blend into the landscape and set his traps again."

"You're calling him guilty, Mr. Chappell, without knowing all the facts. What are you going to do if you find him?"

"Whatever is necessary to protect myself."

"Sounds like you're trying for prison, Mr. Chappell. This is no gun fight at high noon or whatever you have in mind. You know where to look for him?"

"The phone book. If he's not at his office or home, I'll ask my girlfriend—his ex-wife. She should know if he's got a hide-away."

"Your best bet would be to drop the girlfriend."

"Drop my girlfriend? You could tell me where Dr. Alexander is and make it a lot easier."

"We're not tracking him, Mr. Chappell. If I were sure where he was, telling you, in theory, might make it easier on you, maybe not. If he's not where he lives, you break into his place without his permission, and you're asking for jail. Look, Alexander's got no police record. Generally, Dr. Alexander comes across as a solid enough citizen. A little strange, maybe. He pushed you around a little, but that doesn't make him a criminal in the eyes of the law. I'll bet you've pushed a few people around. We all do. Okay, Dr. Rudy treated Johnston. But that doesn't mean that he put Johnston on to you. Think about who else might also want to get to you."

Detective Byrne got up, ready to leave.

"One last word, detective. Crime and law are like the running of a school: law combines what a principal and a janitor do, the top and the bottom of it. The law sets the example with the threat of authority. At the same time, the law cleans up the mistakes that people make."

"So?"

"So, the law doesn't necessarily help much between the gap

where crime goes on. The law beyond threats does little to prevent the anarchy of private lives, and that's where the blood is shed, there and in war. It was in that anarchy, I'll bet, that Earl Johnston died. Where was the law when Johnston attacked me? I'm caught in that same private anarchy, and there's nothing you can do about it, detective."

"Sorry you're so bitter, Mr. Chappell. You might go to church. That's the best solution to the problem you describe. Anyway, thanks for the beer. Please keep in touch."

It was late. I phoned Edith, who proved to be testy at my late departure from *Jupiter*. So, I drove in haste, concentrating on getting back to Edith quickly. Despite this distraction and concern, I got to thinking about Dr. Rudolpho Alexander and the Johnstons, new people in my life, people whom I would never see grow old, never think of as friends.

My route to Edith's took me along the country road from which Rudy had tried and failed to force me off the road. Part of the feeling that had come to me after the attack, when I had returned to *Jupiter* and was watching the night from *Jupiter*, came back again, particularly the feeling that the disorder with which I was contending derived from "a plague of surrogates." I was contending with symbols, with masks. I had little first-hand feel for what the Johnstons and Rudy were up to, why they lived, and how they had changed. There had to be more to Rudy and

Pappy and Mae than just an appetite for ownership and a thirst for blood. The only reason why I had any interest in Rudy was his grudge against me; the Johnstons served as a potential means for my protection. I could only guess at what the lives of Pappy and Mae had been before we had met. Now, my ignorance of their lives made it hard for me to use them for my protection. My need to know about them without really wanting to know produced an uncomfortable irony.

Even Edith represented something of a mask. She stood then for a large part of my future, but I probably knew her no better than, as it turned out, I had known my wife by the time we got our divorce. The best of my prospects with Edith appeared to be a durable enigma: love and need without much knowledge. Given the changeable and furtive motives and appearances of people, how can you tell which parts of a person you know and which you don't? Well, I was depressed.

Anyway, the possibility of a hideaway produced an heir: the further possibility that Rudy might be hiding out at Earl's wedding gift cottage. No end of crazy possibilities. Anyway, the trip with the Johnston family could indeed be fruitful.

As I drove closer to Edith's condo, I considered my next moves. Dr. Rudy could not be anticipated with any certainty. He would probably try to see Edith again, and probably take another crack at me, all of which would have to be handled as seemed right at the moment. If Rudy went into hiding, the better to hatch his plots, then protective custody would be called for Edith and me, say a week on the boat in the south of Chesapeake Bay. No one could find us there. Edith and I could think about what we might do and maybe come up with a new way of resolving our problem with Rudy. For the moment, however, I had to press Edith again for more information about Rudy's habits.

Her friend, Melissa, might be useful if I could lull her ambitions toward Rudy, whatever they were, assuming I read her right. She could also provide leads to Rudy's whereabouts, having known him and Edith when they had been married. Perhaps Melissa Kilmur would remember a once rented cottage by the Chesapeake or in the misty heights of the Blue Ridge, the site of a pleasant weekend, possibly before Melissa's husband had died, and maybe before the trouble between Edith and Rudy had provoked their divorce a while back—a quiet, relaxing weekend among four friends. Come to think of it, given Dr. Rudy's obsession for her, it was probably Edith who acted to gain her divorce, which showed strength of character. How did that strength fit into her life then?

On reconsideration, however, there was little hope that I would learn much from Melissa. She regarded me at least as an intruder, or so I thought. Melissa either resented me for what she thought bad form on my part; or, to her mind, she believed I had taken advantage of a lovers' quarrel between Rudy and Edith, despite their divorce. How much influence did Melissa have over Rudy? What plans and strategies did she have in mind for him? Money? Rudy was rich. You would think that my interest in Edith would further any intimate plans that Melissa might have had towards Rudy, by moving Edith further from Rudy's grasp. A close game was being played here. There were a good many half-seen, subtle parts to Melissa—not to mention Rudy—that I could not tell which way Melissa inclined or what her motives were, other than that she was cool and manipulative.

I looked for a parking space near Edith's condo and considered one last speculation. Once again, I was nearing a jumping-off place in my life: soon, I would have to decide whether take another try at domesticity, this time with Edith. Our recent adventures together had to raise the question of how serious we were about each other. You could be only so casual toward someone who cared enough about you to try to help save your life, having slept with you. The feelings had become shaped, as far as I was concerned—shaped and less casual and less to be taken for granted.

Yet, my past spoke to me of caution. I had been divorced for years. Oddly, now and then, some of the old passion that I had carried for my wife returned, the wish for a settled life. Did Edith feel the same lingering affection for Rudy, even though she denied any such feelings toward him? Occasionally, I sensed tenderness in her toward him. The durability of love and affection was understandable. Yet, why had she married Rudy in the first place? Why did she require the on and off intensity of attention paid by Rudy? And, by me?

~

I was spooked enough to consider for a moment that the lobby of Edith's condo building would be as good a site for an ambush as any, even though it was empty, except for the greeter behind the desk. He was a young, black man, clean cut, pleasant, and neatly attired in his Nehru jacket. He was sitting behind the lobby's all-purpose counter, managing the telephone switchboard for the condo, and introducing guests. He waved me on, for I had become familiar to him and to others on the condo house staff.

I found my ambush all right when I entered Edith's apartment. However, the ambush came from what should have been a friendly quarter, Edith. Her weapon, a tongue heated by anger. Her causes: once again, I was late, had a poor excuse so far as she was concerned, and had to be undependable. For a moment, I wondered if Edith had been talking with my ex-wife, for they shared the same list of my misbehavior—enhanced unreliability—that I had committed.

"Robert! Damn it! You never get anywhere in life because you don't give a damn for anyone else. First, I try to help you by going to that Tilghman place, and you disappear. I've had supper ready for almost two hours. You're as bad as Rudy. The two of you take an unbelievable amount of care... or self-abnegation. I don't believe my luck in men."

I reverted to one of the bad habits I had when married and corked off right back, without thinking: "If this is your idea of taking care of someone, Edith, you should work for the Mafia."

Given Edith's drive for the old Onwards and Upward, I should have expected a rebuke of this sort sooner or later. Edith got me so angry that the only thing I could do then, beyond thinking of leaving, was to find answers that would free me: free me from the plans that Rudy had for me and that would explain why Earl Johnston had assaulted me. Without Edith's information, my chief lead remained Earl Johnston's cottage, which wasn't much of a lead. Maybe as soon as I left Edith, however, my problems with Rudy might stop. Then again, maybe not.

Edith wore mixed expressions on her face: anger and frustration, as well as strain and anxiety. So, reflecting that one of these days someone has got to write a song entitled, "One More Time," I stopped short and asked, "What's really eating you?"

"Beats me, Robert. Between you and Rudy, I don't know what to do. I'm sorry I lost my temper. You did call to say you would be late, and I appreciate that. I guess I'm just depressed. You put aside one set of problems when you leave one person, and you take up another set with someone else."

"Am I really that bad? ...Is that waitress still bothering you?"

"A little. It's also that, in a sense, I'm to blame for Rudy's problems. If I hadn't left him, he wouldn't have lost his cool."

"So, you want to go back to him and take your chances on staying alive?"

"I don't think I want to live with him again... As for murder...?"

"You're too close to this, Edith. Let's leave town. No forwarding address. We'll spend a week on *Jupiter*, away from everything, and you'll have plenty of time to sort this out. No one to press you. Rudy can't follow us because he doesn't know the water."

"Let's get ready to eat, Robert... I've got complications which I'll tell you about."

We spent the next few minutes in silence while Edith finished preparing supper. The interlude gave me a chance to consider one reason that I cared for Edith, her style, which showed to best advantage in efforts such as setting a fine table. With an economy of time and effort, she would cook a meal: on this occasion, fish sautéd to perfection (somehow rescued from overdone) upon my arrival, crisp peas, and a salad with a surprise or two in it (feta cheese, a few bites of ham and bacon, Greek olives, and Boston lettuce). She also anticipated one of my liabilities by producing a bottle of Sauvé from the icebox after I apologized for forgetting to bring the wine that I usually brought. We sat down at the table to a meal in the setting of dark brown napkins next to Lennox China, and crystal, all resting on a summer blue sky table cloth, with candles illuminating the scene.

"Does my lack of active ambition bother you?" I asked.

"Sometimes. I guess I saw it as a handle for beating you with, just now."

"What are the complications for our getting away?"

"For one thing, Melissa's in trouble. She's quite concerned. Agnes has been gone for a couple days. It's not like Agnes."

"From the little I saw of it, Melissa rode her hard. She treated Agnes badly."

"Why do you always look for the dark side of things, Robert? Melissa may get edgy now and then, but, basically, she's kind and considerate. Agnes is devoted to her, I'm sure of it."

"What do you think happened to Agnes? Do you think that Rudy might have something to do with it?"

"I can't see why. Why did you say that?"

"He's nuts. He may have figured another off-the-wall ploy for getting you back and eliminating me."

"Well, Rudy did get carried away when he tried to run you off the road. Maybe he even treated Mr. Johnston... I don't know. But, frankly, Robert, it's a long way from roughing a rival to out and out murder. All you have are suspicions when it comes to the murderer. How do you know that Rudy has been trying to kill you? The most certain thing you know about him is that you dislike him."

"And he, me," I responded.

To which she responded: "I've known Rudy better and longer than you, and I'm a good enough judge of character to have picked you as a friend and lover. Rudy can be petty, willful, and even violent, but no more so than any other man... or woman. I still believe that he's an experimenter, but no killer. My God, Robert, I've slept with him as a wife."

"The trouble that you and I..."

"You! Robert. You're the one who sees the trouble and the big picture."

"Are you with me in this, or not?"

"Of course, I am. But you jump to conclusions too easily. First, you conclude that something out of your past was responsible for the attack on *Jupiter*. Then you conclude that the attack came out of my past. Why can't there be a little Nasty Chance at work? I've considered your conclusions, and, frankly, my dear, they don't seem to be based much on fact."

"How can I figure out what's going on when I don't even know the basic facts? You, for example. I still don't know much about your past. Nothing in mine explains what's happening."

"What do you want to know?" she asked, sighing.

"Did you and Rudy have any favorite places that he might use as a hideout?"

Edith smiled before saying, "You men are after only one thing—the solution to your problems. Apart from Rudy's house or his office, I don't know where he'd be. If the police were really after Rudy, you would think they'd ask me that question, not you?"

"Didn't you and Rudy ever go off to any place for the weekend? A cabin?"

"Rarely. He was so devoted to his work—single-minded then—we didn't go many places. There was one time. It was on the Eastern Shore. A cabin. There was a small river outside the back door—I think we were near the headwaters of the Choptank, near the Delaware border. Rudy said the cabin belonged to one of his patients. It was a pigsty. We did not stay there."

"Was this when Rudy was working for the sanitarium, Health-Wood?"

"I believe so. You don't think… Johnston didn't have money enough for that, did he?"

"It may not be the same place. Was this one of the weekends when you were thinking of leaving Rudy?"

"In fact, it was a weekend when I was thinking of returning to him."

"Returning to him? When we were first dating, Edith, you used to drop out of sight for days and even for a week or so. Were you going back to Rudy?"

"Usually. Does it make a difference? You and I were simply lovers. You were not a responsibility then."

"Now?"

"More and more. It's one of the things I must figure out… Do I really want to settle down again?"

"The cabin," I said, "do you remember anything unusual about it?"

"Mostly that it was a terrible mess. I even cleaned up a little of it, the worst parts. Also, a door to one of the rooms was locked. I found a key to it. Of all things, it was the bathroom. It was huge. It had a shower big enough for several people or a first-class S&M orgy for people who like to hurt themselves, or others." Edith, smiling, then asked, "Do you think the cottage might have been Bluebeard's castle, 20th-century style?"

"Could be. How can I find the cottage?"

"I can't really say. I don't remember how to get there. It was near a small town named Greensboro. That's all I remember."

"Are there any other places that Rudy might go to?"

"You've tried his house?"

"No... but, I've thought about it but was advised against it by the police."

"Melissa's the only other possibility. With Agnes gone, she may not be responsive. She thinks you've got Rudy all wrong. Anyway, I'll come with you to Melissa's. That might help."

A phone call to Melissa produced yet another invitation for talk and dessert. It would be an informal meal because of her lack of help. I said nothing about it at the time to Edith but, so far as I could see, there was no telling what might have happened to Agnes, barring the chance that she had reverted to type and foresworn slavery in the midst of wealth for a return to a simple country life again.

Edith and I walked down the hall toward Melissa's condo. The hallway served one purpose: access to the condos on the third floor. The design of the hall denied any distraction, any food or game for the mind, such as windows. Anyway, where could windows be put? What about providing a view into the condos along the hall, a view into the slow and quiet lives of John and Mary Doe? Perhaps they could be caught making love on the living room floor. Or perhaps in a family battle royal at the dinner table, if the windows from the hall into their condos were one way. So, the Does could see only reflections of themselves on the mirrored panes of one-way glass. The halls to Melissa could be live theater. Maybe windows in the hall—if it served as an outside wall—could look out onto the city, onto local backyards and alleys. But the designer of the hall could well argue that the city's intestines hardly offered an uplifting, aesthetic sight.

If not windows in the hallway to Melissa's condo, then why not paintings or photographs? The Great Designer probably felt that the citizens of the hall and its condos, starved for profit and alert for booty, would steal such art. Or, these citizens could just as easily deface such art, giving in to the thrill of the moment, or perhaps lodge a protest against the Evil or Oppression of the moment.

Edith and I were walking in a modern Anyplace. The hallway could be at any high-efficiency spot on earth and there would be no way of telling where we were because of the anonymity of the place. The hall could even be submerged in the ocean, maybe even part of an enormous research institute devoted to checking out the ocean floor for life, manganese, and maybe even a little gold. My reveries dissipated before Melissa's door. I knocked. The peephole winked with light and darkness. Melissa opened the door and beckoned us in.

"Do come in. Sorry for the Spartan style."

"Any word on Agnes?" Edith asked as we were shepherded toward the dining room. Rudy was nowhere in sight.

"None whatsoever," Melissa replied.

Little had changed in the dining room; the flight of help apparently having made little practical difference in the running of the place. The table was set much as before. Appearances grew thin when Melissa excused herself and went into the kitchen, and, sure enough, she reappeared after a couple of minutes carrying a tray with two saucers on it, each saucer supporting a larger piece of German chocolate cake.

"Your skill at cooking is amazing, Melissa."

"Thank you, Edith. You're a dear."

"I still can't get over Agnes," Edith continued.

"Neither can I, dear. We did have an exchange of words this morning. At the time, I didn't think much of it. I went out at lunch. When I returned, Agnes had gone without leaving a note or anything, and it just is not like her. She has always left a note when she's left and I haven't been here. I haven't had a chance to get to the bank, and I owe Agnes a couple of weeks of back wages. Do you suppose that that might have had something to do with her disappearance? I said I'd pay her back. You'd think she'd want a good reference."

"Not all that much time has passed. Chances are she'll show up. Anyway, it doesn't sound as if she was abducted," I said.

"It's just not like her," Melissa replied. "She is the soul of conscientiousness and punctuality."

"Is anything missing?" I asked.

"No. I don't think so."

I continued, "Do you think she went out shopping and got mugged on the way back? She might be in a hospital. Is that what you are afraid of?"

"No. There's no reason for her to be abducted, that I know of. To be crude, Agnes is too ugly to be raped and too poor to be robbed. I have checked with the police, and they know nothing. Beyond that, I have no idea what has happened to her," Melissa responded.

"Do you know where Agnes comes from?" Edith queried.

"I have the address of her parents. Akron, Ohio. And, I think there's a letter from her daughter."

"Daughter? She didn't look old enough," I interjected.

"No. She doesn't look her age. But having her daughter probably added to her country looks," Melissa responded. "Enough of my problems. The two of you should know something. Rudy left here about half an hour ago. It seems that the police have been looking for him, and he decided to go to them before they came to him."

"Where's he going?" I asked.

"A police station, somewhere in Annapolis, I believe," Melissa replied.

"Why are the police looking for him?" I asked.

"Don't be cute, Robert. Rudy says he's innocent of his patient's murder—Earl Johnston. I believe Rudy. He has had terrible luck in the past couple of years. Ever since my husband died, really. Ever since the divorce occurred... excuse me, Edith."

Edith gave a start at the mention of the divorce.

"Also, Robert," Melissa continued, "there's the question of

your complaint against Rudy. Are you pressing it?"

"Why not?"

"Well, Rudy had the—what do you call it?—a tube-fence or pulpit to your boat repaired. *Jupiter*?"

"That's the name."

"Why hold a grudge, Robert?"

"The name of the game is defense, lady, not offense," I said.

"Don't get hostile, Robert. What are you talking about?"

"Rudy tried to kill me, not vice versa."

Edith cut in, saying, "You don't know that! I agree; it looks bad. But, Rudy's impulsive, not evil. He shouldn't have tried to run you off the road, but I really don't think he wanted to kill you. He just wanted to scare you, the same way as when he damaged your pulpit."

"The yard said nothing about it to me!" I replied.

"But," Edith responded, "the pulpit's been repaired! Right?"

"Right! We are in a play in which the main action takes place backstage," I said.

"It was Rudy's stupid warning to you. He confessed to that and has paid for the repairs, in case he or the yard haven't told you. You and I have already discussed the attack on the boat, and after thinking about it, I believe that Melissa's right. Both of us know Rudy. You don't. Trust our judgment and give him a break."

"Before I decide," I concluded, "I'll talk to the police and see what they have to say."

When Edith and I returned to her condo, I phoned Detective Byrne. He had gone off duty. It was getting late, but even so, Edith and I settled down for a quiet game of honeymoon bridge. We had played only a few hands when she complained of an upset stomach and a sharp headache. Her symptoms worsened quickly. Taking no chances, I drove her to the emergency room of a nearby hospital, where after a short wait, she was admitted. The diagnosis? A mild case of food poisoning. Her doctor could not say, however, whether Melissa's dessert had been the cause. I had asked whether the chocolate cake had caused the poisoning because, even though I was okay after eating the same cake, I was getting so paranoid that I was suspecting everyone of everything. The doctor at the hospital wanted Edith to stay for the rest of the night and perhaps the next day for observation.

After leaving Edith, I decided to check my apartment for mail and intruders. I was on edge. Edith's illness and the disappearance of Agnes, however doubtful that seemed at the time, were the latest bad omens. They intimated—given the mood I was in—that some disaster stood just around the next darkened corner, ready to step out and startle me by introducing itself violently.

Was another ambush in the works for me? Before entering my apartment, I had taken the precaution of going to the back of it and looking up at the windows to my place. They were dark. When I thought about it, the darkness did not really indicate whether anyone was in there, for an ambush would be best launched in the dark. Time to get on with it, I took the stairs to the second floor.

Again, I got cautious. To make any ambush planned for me sporting, I paused at my door and listened. No sound. I knocked loudly on the door and, feeling a little silly, cried out in a deep voice, "Mr. Chappell! Are you in there!?" I hoped to confuse anyone who might be waiting when I walked in, and to give myself time either to get out quickly or to attack. The only thing I could hear, however, was the sound of combat from a television shoot 'em up from outside my apartment, from some nest down the hall.

I knocked again. No response. I inserted my key into the lock, opened the door quickly, and flipped on the light switch next to the door. A great flash burst into the room from the light on the ceiling, a quiet explosion in brilliance, like a brief airburst over Vietnam at night.

My reflexes were so ragged, and I was so tensed up that I jumped into the room and onto the floor to chew dirt and slammed the door shut while doing so. I lay for a few moments in the dark, listening and hearing only the sounds of the hall. I felt my way slowly to a nearby table with a lamp on it. When I turned the light on, would I see the body of the good maid

Agnes, a prop for setting me up for her murder? Or, maybe Rudy sat in the darkened room, gun in hand, ready to speed me towards Judgment Day. Well, I took a chance and turned on the light, only to find that all was normal.

My couch was still threadbare. The carpet near the door was still worn, showing the path I took when my life was normal and I was going to or returning from work. The worn places in the rug were as familiar as a family dog, waiting for the return of the master of the house. Someday, I would have to lay out money for improving the décor. At a minimum, I'd have to replace the blown light bulb in the ceiling. What a time for it to go.

Now, though, I was happy enough, what with no corpse or assailant in sight. I was in the odd position of feeling I'd done right by being cautious while still feeling that I was a fool, that anyone who had witnessed my behavior would have thought me a fool. That said, the possibility of the potential threat in my apartment backed off, with everything being in place as it was.

CHAPTER 10

Earl's House

New day, new prospects. A good night's sleep made for a calm mind and a steady pace. I phoned Edith and found her in chipper spirits. She expected to be released from the hospital by the end of the day, in time for Saturday night. I pointed out that there would still be time for the two of us to get off together on *Jupiter*. She responded by suggesting that I buy food for our excursion, maybe a little extra, in case we decided to stay over Monday. I phoned Detective Byrne, but he wasn't due in until noon, so I would have to wait a little longer to get a better idea of how Rudy stood with the police.

While eating breakfast, I looked over my checkbook and found a petty cash shortage. Time to return to work. Not much more I could do about investigating the sources of my recent adventures beyond checking out the Earl Johnston memorial cabin. I phoned my boss, brought her up to date, heard her say, "Don't worry, clear up your problem and come in when you can. But, as soon as you can turn your adventures into a news story or feature, please file it. Phone me if necessary." It would be Tuesday that I'd be in, I said, maybe Wednesday at the latest. What a rare tolerance she displayed among newspaper bosses. My financial health assured for the near future; it was time to leave for the Johnstons in the land across the Bay.

A cold rain fell as I walked to my car. The end of autumn had come. Most of the recent splendor had washed from the trees, leaving in view a multitude of blackened veins against a dour sky. However grim the sky and cold the rain, it was still too early for winter by a month or so, judging by the calendar. Of course, a calendar would not necessarily indicate a change in season, for a calendar was just a system, a kind of grid, that people held up against the changes in Nature over which they had no immediate control. So far as the seasons went, a calendar proved most useful for a person who avoided going outside, or if he or she were so lost in concerns as to ignore changes in temperature, the length of days, the colors of the world, and even now and then migrant birds on their way. In my car, I tuned in a weather forecast: fair skies by the afternoon, with the arrival of a warm front.

As arranged, I stopped by the Rudd Yard to pick up Nestor. No show. No one knew where he was, nor had anyone seen him yet at the yard.

I waited for a half-hour without success before resuming my drive without him. On the way to Tilghman, I wondered if I were on a local version of a snipe hunt. Had the Johnstons out-foxed me? They could be sure now of my arriving no sooner than 10:30 in the morning, because of my arrangement with Nestor. Given my paranoia, I wondered whether Pappy, Mae, and Nestor Johnston were preparing some squirrelly surprise for me. More likely, the Johnstons were checking over the cabin before putting it up for sale or putting the cabin to some other purpose, such as using it themselves. By standing me up, Nestor raised the question of how dependable he was. Yet, he might have gotten on the wrong side of unforeseen circumstances.

High above the Chesapeake, from the half way point of the Bay Bridge, I could see the Eastern Shore spread out. It was a tableau: a study in the Payne's grey of the Chesapeake and its marshes, and the burnt ochres and siennas, and blacks and dark purples of the land, beneath a dirty cotton ball sky. The rear-view mirror reflected an edge of the cloud cover and, beyond that edge, the cerulean promise of a sunny day after all, good news coming in from the West, a carrying out of the radio weather forecast prophecy. Paranoia from the attacks on me from Johnston and Dr. Rudy relaxed some of its hold on me. As memories, those incidents were becoming ghosts, gone mostly but not forgotten.

When I drove up to the Johnstons' chain-link fortress that guarded the ruins of their house, the gate opened automatically. A nice touch. Only the two Johnstons were there, Pappy and

Mae, standing on their driveway near the ruins of their house.

"Sorry I'm late," I said. "I waited for Nestor, but he never showed."

"That's okay," Pappy said. "Let's go. Nestor felt like riding his cycle over here in the rain and came before you did. He's gone on to the cabin. He'll meet us there, if you're still interested." Pappy smiled as he said that.

"Ready when you are," I replied.

To see how the other twentieth lives, I went with the Johnstons in their Mercedes Benz estate wagon, even though that meant I would go or stay at their pleasure. At their request, I drove.

The drive itself to the cabin grew tedious. Apart from an exchange of directions now and then, the Johnstons and I rode in silence, as if in meditation at a Quaker Sunday meeting, waiting for someone to speak from inner light. Another line of my meditations presented itself: Edith's anger at my lapse with the waitress. My lapse was over and done with. In view of her own vacations from my company, Edith could hardly bear much of a grudge against me about the matter; and, in fact, I had high hopes that the planets and stars would move to a favorable position, and Edith and I would mend our differences over the weekend.

The stands of tall trees and flat fields near the Bay as we headed inland toward the center of the Delmarva Peninsula delivered tableland, field after field, post-harvest, and drab. At one point when the view outside offered nothing of interest and when the ride had become monotonous, I turned to Pappy and told him the Mercedes handled well.

"It should," he said. "It cost enough."

"How much?"

"Enough. You're probably wondering how an Army man could afford it and a large, quickly built fence around my place."

I said nothing.

"I invested my money wisely," he continued. "For one thing, Mae used to work in a bank, and banks know as well as anyone where the future lies. That's the secret to success. If you're not smart enough to figure out for yourself what's going to happen, get near someone who makes his living knowing what the future will be."

"Is there any chance that Mae might have made some enemies in her job?" I asked, mildly curious. "If so, one of them might have killed Earl."

"No," Mae said from the back seat. "Usually, I keep to myself."

"Mae don't make no enemies." Pappy followed, saying, "You surely have a powerful interest in my son's death. Mr. Chappell, is there anything more to your concern than what you've told us?"

"What do you mean?" I asked.

"Nothing," Pappy replied. "I'm the one who makes the enemies, me… and Earl. He was just like me. It was his enemies or mine that killed him."

A mile or so short of Greensboro, Maryland, we had forsaken the highway for an obscure, twisting, and beat-up side road, topped with dirt and gravel. The road became two parallel paths through a meadow. At the end of the final transformation, a few last yards of path through tall grass brought the three of us to the Earl Johnston estate: cabin and weed patch. The estate offered a near view of the Choptank River a short way from the back door, running fifty yards wide of water that looked brackish and stagnant. What a difference in the river. At its mouth, miles downstream, the Choptank opened wide as it approached Chesapeake Bay and its brackish waters.

It could not have cost Pappy and Mae a fortune to buy the cabin. From the outside it looked like a large hunting shack. Considering the money apparent in the Mercedes and the chain-link palisade, the Johnston elders had hardly gone all out for young Earl.

I looked around for a symbol of Nestor's wealth, his motorcycle, and saw it near the rear of the shack, resting upright on its stand. Here and there swatches of tall grass hung from its frame, token from a ride through the meadow. Had Nestor been even more shortchanged in the Johnston fortunes? After all, given his relative poverty, appearances suggested that Nestor hardly qualified as a favorite son. Probably no report about that until Nestor married, if he married.

I looked for some indication that Rudy might be present, in

case he should put in as unlikely an appearance here as he had at Melissa's. The drying mud of part of the path from the meadow held fresh tire tracks. It was time for the ritual tire track comparison. A quick check worthy of any second-rate detective showed that the tire tread in the mud differed in design from the tire tread on the Johnston's car and, in fact, was wide enough to be from a small truck, maybe a van or pickup.

"Have the police been here?" I asked Pappy and Mae, as the three of us stood before the cabin.

Pappy looked as if he had been stung. "Why did you ask that?" he demanded.

"The tire tracks," I replied. "The ones in the mud here are different from the ones on your car."

He came over and crouched to get a closer look. Pappy may have looked old, but he moved young. No sign of arthritis, fragile bones, or stiff muscles for him.

"Could have been the cops here," he said. "Don't know how they could have found out about this place. Earl wouldn't have told them."

"They didn't look it over as part of their murder investigation?" I asked.

"Why should the cops come here?" he said, irritated. "This is miles away from where Earl was found and probably miles more from where he was murdered."

"The story in the newspaper said Earl's body was found at Knapp's Narrows. There was nothing written about where the murder took place. Couldn't Earl have been killed someplace else, like here, and dumped where he was found?"

"You wouldn't be the killer coming up here to see if your tracks was covered, would you?" Pappy asked, displaying a sick smile.

"If I was, I sure got around."

"You sure do."

"Yea… after Earl attacked me, I jumped into his boat, told him all was forgiven, and made friends with him. He liked me so much that he took me here to show off the place at midnight. We got drunk. I killed him because he had more money than I did and because he beat me at pinochle."

"Very funny. What you say? I'm a mean son of a bitch. How do I know Earl attacked you?"

"Check the police for my report to them. Or ask my girl-friend. She was there on my boat, trying to make Earl and me friends. If you think she's a lying hooker, then check with the two restaurants where Earl tried to strike up a friendship in St. Michaels by dumping chowder and beer on me. Earl liked me so much that he left his favorite knife with me on my boat for safe keeping."

"Was that a fillet knife, Mr. Chappell?" Mae asked.

"Yes."

"Shit! Who has it?" Pappy asked.

"The cops. It's evidence."

"That's my fucking knife. I told Earl not to take it. You better be nice to me, Chappell, or you walk home if you're lucky."

I couldn't tell if Pappy was angry at my assault on his pride, about the mention of his son, or about the loss of his knife. Either way, he was angry. Time to get on with it.

The inside of the main room of the cabin suggested the disorder of its owner's mind. The disorder indicated some of the casual violence and minor chaos that marked Earl's life. A couple of squat chairs and a couch represented the style and theme of the room. The stuffing of the couch and chairs protruded here and there through worn, gray, herniated, outer cloth: injuries resulting from gentle blows through the years of many bodies sitting, squirming, shifting about, and rising from the cloth flesh of the couch and chairs. Dust and dirt lay undisturbed on windowsills, corners, and on a couple of old tables, away from the main routes of foot traffic. A rug covered up much of the floor, a rug that had probably served time in a motel room somewhere and that had been denied release from servitude. The rug served a noble purpose insofar as it hid much of the dark, old, pine planked floor that was short on varnish, and maybe long on splinters. Rounding out the scene were a pole lamp with a tarnished fake brass finish and two ceramic-based table lamps probably salvaged on garbage pickup day, from a front lawn in the suburbs.

Nestor walked into the room, said hello, and apologized for standing me up, saying that he'd changed his mind. He came from what appeared to be a large bathroom with a shower big enough to provide for at least six people at one time, probably the room that Edith had found locked, if this was the cabin she had recalled. Bright red tiles lined the top of the shower walls.

"Well, what do you think of Earl's bathroom?" Nestor asked me. "Ain't it a whopper?"

"Never seen anything like it… in a private house."

"Earl had it built onto the cabin just a few months ago. Mae and Pappy gave it to him as a birthday present," he continued.

I looked around the bathroom and noticed stainless steel rings embedded into the walls of the shower near the ceiling, which was also tiled, but in a cream color. "What are the rings for?" I asked Nestor.

Pappy, who had come to the door of the bathroom, looked at the rings and said, "Don't know. Earl said something about wanting to butcher deer and other game here, though why he wouldn't have done that outside, I don't know. The rings could hold the carcass off the floor."

I looked at Pappy closely, but he did not change his expression. "The rings wouldn't have been part of the equipment Dr. Alexander recommended for Earl's treatment, would they?" I asked.

"Chappell, you're a pain in the ass, and you're getting on my nerves," Pappy snapped before continuing with, "what Earl did with Dr. Alexander, Mae and I don't know."

Mae came to the door too and said, "Mr. Chappell, you are our guest here. We have put ourselves out for your curiosity. You seem to have forgotten that."

"I'm sorry. I don't mean to cause either of you any more grief or trouble. I forgot where I was because of my own concerns."

Silence fell. The Johnstons had caused me to pull back. Even so, when I took another look at the red tiles of the showers and the rings and even the stainless-steel sink in the room, I could not help but think that it might have served Earl Johnston and the experimental Dr. Rudy as an ideal place for applying a little torture here and there.

When I returned to the main room, I went over the couch and, giving way to curiosity, pulled up the cushions and found two dimes and a penny. Under the cushion of one of the chairs, I came up with a broach, like the one that I'd seen Agnes wear when I had first visited Melissa. The broach was something missing from someone missing: the scrimshaw whale still tossed the whaling boat full of men toward heaven. Why was the broach there? Neither Mae, Pappy, nor Nestor admitted to ever seeing the broach before, and didn't think that it belonged to Earl, because he had not taken up with any woman that they had known of since his release from jail and the start of his treatments with Dr. Alexander. There was a weak possibility that Agnes, on loan for some unexplained reason from Melissa, might have come here with the good doctor after Earl's death.

I described Agnes to the Johnstons and asked if Dr. Rudy had ever shown up with her. No, they replied, though on a couple of occasions he had brought with him an older, refined woman; out of Earl's class. Mae's description suggested Lady Melissa Kilmur. Where had they seen this woman, at their place or here in the cabin? Both places, they replied. Had Rudy ever brought along a young woman, his wife? Nope, they replied.

It took a couple more hours for the Johnstons to go over the rest of the place. I'd exhausted my possibilities well before they did. I'd found nothing more of interest, no mass grave outside, no bloodstains on the inside. Pappy and Mae discussed what to do with the cabin. It was a conversation they admitted to having had several times during the past few days; and, in fact, our trip, to the two of them, seemed to have been undertaken to produce a decision about the cabin. In the end, they decided, with some reluctance, to give it to Nestor if he really wanted it. They talked as they did within Nestor's hearing. He did want the cabin.

The chill that followed my questions about the rings on the bathroom wall eased. In fact, Mae even offered me a cup of coffee. I declined. From stores and equipment in the cabin, the Johnstons brewed their coffee and drank it. Eventually, after a couple of other delays, the four of us left this sad cabin, Nestor by his means and the three of us by car.

I raced the sun and lost: it disappeared beyond the horizon before I reached the Bay Bridge. I pulled off the road at a gas station a couple of miles onto the Western Shore and phoned Edith, back at her place. I told her that, so long as I was near Annapolis, I'd stop by Detective Byrne's office—even if it was Sunday and he should be off work—to find out what had happened with Rudy. She said fine. She'd gotten healthy enough to cook supper for us and was happy enough to hold off serving it for a while yet. At the barracks, I learned that Byrne was not there, so I asked for and found Neil Saugers, the other detective on the Johnston case.

Saugers stood when I walked over to his desk. His height probably made him the joy (it would take a lot of cloth to fit him) and the despair (tall and thin as he was, who could fit him?) of your average custom, Savile-Row tailor. I was thinking nonsense. At Saugers' salary, he probably shopped at down-the-street, off-the-rack haberdasher. No finely tailored executive boardroom ambitions for this man. I liked him even though, at second glance, he looked like a giant, mournful, praying mantis the way he hunched over what he was looking at, his hands clasped in front. He differed from Byrne, a man held in thrall by doing the job right. If appearances proved out, Saugers would fit into any circumstances well because he remained at ease with himself, or so it seemed. When I introduced myself, he broke into a broad smile and gave me a friendly handshake as I started to explain my reason for seeking him out.

"Sit down here, Mr. Chappell. So… you're still the same as when we met on the docks in Galesville, and I asked you about Earl Johnston. I take it that you're on a mission. Is the information you're after for publication or for private?"

"It's private. I came partly to get information and partly to give it."

"Sounds good. What've you got?"

"I visited a cabin that Earl Johnston owned. Do you know about it?"

"Just found out about it. The father of the deceased phoned a short while ago and said we might want to look at it. Mr. Pappy Johnston didn't think it had any connection with the murder. That's why he didn't say anything about it before now. That's his story. What do you think, Mr. Chappell?"

"I think he's wrong, but I don't have evidence to prove it. You know that Earl Johnston was a mess... a sadist and God knows what else."

"Maybe. We're still investigating."

I told Saugers of my suspicions about how Earl had used his cabin, and about finding the broach and its significance, so far as I knew it. I went on to explain how Earl's parents had seen a woman resembling Melissa, with Earl and Rudy, which raised the possibility that Melissa's maid had likewise been to the cabin, though not to clean up. Agnes was missing. I left the broach under the cushion where I had found it. Saugers said he might check the cabin out the next day, Sunday.

"What about Dr. Rudy?" I asked.

"We questioned him again and let him go. Had to. We're considering your complaint against him. I'll grant you that the doctor is a touch spooky. But spooky is not enough for us to hold him. The law doesn't take spooky into account."

"What would you do in my situation?" I asked.

"I'd dump the girl and be on the alert. Are you thinking of dropping your complaint against the doctor? He seemed to think you might."

"That depends partly on you're feeling about the case."

"What do you mean?" Saugers asked.

"If you guys think Dr. Rudy killed Earl but don't have enough evidence to prove it, my complaint could be a way of keeping a line on him until you check out the case completely."

"Can I call you Robert?"

"Sure."

"Call me Neil. We don't know that your doctor killed Johnston. The tip about the cabin may help us, so I'll get on it right away. We'll also see this Melissa you're talking about, Robert."

"Melissa Kilmur. She goes by Lady Kilmur. She says her late husband was a wannabe aristocrat. I'll give you her address."

"Yea. Check back with me tomorrow afternoon. I may know something more. Just to play it safe, don't drop the complaint yet."

CHAPTER 11

Discovery

"Supper will be ready in just a minute, Robert," Edith said as I took off my jacket. "A strange thing happened before you came," she continued. "There's a Mrs. Agilesto who lives down the hall, across from Melissa. Have I ever introduced you to her?"

"No."

"I don't know her well, but she likes me. She visited me an hour or so ago while I was starting supper, and she told me the strangest story about Melissa."

"What's that?"

A knock interrupted her before she could give me an answer. Was Mrs. Agilesto at the door for a return engagement? No. At Edith's request, I opened the door and found Melissa.

"May I come in, Robert?" Melissa asked. She stood there as rigid as if carved from ice, and she glared at me.

"Sure. Come on in."

Edith came from the kitchen, carrying the main dish for supper, a casserole. "Melissa…" she began.

It was awkward. Edith had been about to tell a strange story about Melissa; Melissa looked angry and wanted to let her anger out. And I just wanted to eat supper.

"Robert," Melissa said, "the police want to talk to me about the murder business you and Edith were involved in."

"Me?" Edith said.

"What I mean to ask, Robert, is whether you had anything to do with this?"

"I didn't commit the murder if that's what you're after."

"Really, Robert, be serious. Did you suggest to Detective Saugers that he contact me?"

"I told him that you accompanied Rudy on some of his visits to Earl Johnston and the Johnston family. I guess Nature has taken its course."

"How do you know that I went along with Rudy?"

"The Johnstons told me."

"They knew who I was?"

"You're a distinctive lady."

"There's no point in my being involved in this, Robert. I am provoked at you for dragging me into this."

"And I'm surprised at you, Melissa. You don't want to help solve the murder? Don't you care?"

"Not really. I didn't really know the man. I accompanied Rudy to keep him company and for the adventure of it all… to learn how things went… that's why I went."

"Why did you go so often?" I asked, fishing for possibilities, for I had no idea how often she had gone. "It couldn't have been much of an adventure after the first couple of times."

"Well, it was an adventure. Rudy needed company, and so did I."

"Earl was strange company. Not a pleasant man, I understand."

"Rudy has a good many patients. You wouldn't be warming me up for the police, would you?" Melissa asked.

"You haven't been sitting in on Rudy's violence therapy sessions, have you?"

"Only as an observer," Melissa responded.

"Uh... Melissa," Edith interjected, "Rudy has said nothing about this..."

"Edith, dear," Melissa replied, "as you know, I've helped Rudy with his investments even before you left him. He was broken up by your departure. He needed support. I am his friend. Nothing more."

Edith cut into the awkward silence that followed by asking Melissa hesitantly if she would like to join us for supper. After hesitating for theatrical effect, Melissa said she would indeed. Nothing shy about her. The final preparations for the meal having been made, we sat down to eat in a silence that was probably uncomfortable for all. After we had sorted out the food and condiments, Melissa said, "The warm spell may be the last time this year that you can go sailing, Robert."

"Yes."

Melissa smiled and, apparently casting about for something acceptable to say, asked, "Do you plan to go sailing tomorrow? It's supposed to be a gorgeous day, except for a chance of rain in the afternoon or evening."

"We might," I responded.

"Might?" Edith said. "I was planning on it."

"Then we will," I answered.

Edith turned to Melissa and asked casually, "Anything new about Agnes?"

"Still no word, my dear."

"It is strange. You haven't… Agnes left… when was it, a couple days ago… and that's it? Not a word?"

"Edith, it's been a long day. Do you think I'd keep anything from you?"

The three of us ate for a while without talking, before Edith said to Melissa, "I didn't know you had gone off with Rudy on his trips. You never said anything to me about it. It sounds like you might have spent more time with him as a friend than I ever did as a wife."

"Edith, I must have said something to you about it. If I didn't, it was only to protect your feelings after the divorce, my dear. I didn't, as you put it, 'go off' with him. I just went along on a few occasions for the companionship. Nothing to worry about."

"Well, I didn't mean, 'go off.' I've mentioned the subject not out of worry. I'm just surprised at the irony of it all. In fact, I'm glad you've watched over Rudy. I've been concerned about him, even though we're no longer married. What was it like, watching him at work?"

"Maybe companionship is the wrong word to describe my relations with Rudy. It has been more like being a guardian to him. After all, as you know, I've been his financial advisor ever since my beloved Charles died, and my protective feelings, I guess, also prompted me to look after Rudy. I was a kind of angel to him. But... to answer your question, I haven't really watched Rudy practice all that much. He is a determined man. He's quite patient in his way. Of course, as we both know, he also can be immature and impulsive now and then. When I've seen him at work, not much that is dramatic has happened, except perhaps for the movies of violence that he would show to people such as Earl Johnston. So far as I can tell, Rudy is an effective doctor."

I asked Melissa, "Did Rudy ever hold any sessions at Earl's house?"

"His house?"

"Yes, the cabin where he lived, near Greensboro, Maryland. Were you ever there?" I followed up.

"I thought you meant Rudy's house. Now that you mention it, I have been there. It's primitive."

"Melissa, I found in Earl Johnston's cabin a broach that Agnes wore the other day."

"What does that have to do with me? I have no idea how it could have gotten there. I wasn't aware that Agnes and Mr. Johnston even knew each other. Strange."

"Then, there's the appointments of the cabin, Melissa. It has quite a bathroom."

"I beg your pardon, Robert. I'm not a connoisseur of bathrooms. To tell the truth, I normally avoid the subject at meals. What peculiar tastes in conversation you have."

Edith joined in, "Why on earth, Robert, are you talking about Earl's bathroom?"

"Edith!" Melissa exclaimed. "Let's not talk anymore about it."

"I brought up the subject," I responded, "because I think it has something to do with Earl's murder."

"I don't care about Earl's murder or anyone else's murder!" Melissa exclaimed.

"I think the bathroom was used as a torture chamber and slaughterhouse."

"And you think," Edith said, "that Rudy had something to do with those things?"

"I can't say for sure yet," I replied, "but he relied on torture as part of his treatment for separating his patients from their violent impulses. I was interested in seeing if Melissa knew anything about it."

"Well, I don't anything about that, apart from observing a couple of his sessions!" squealed Melissa, by now completely angry. "So, this is what the police will be asking me about? You've served quite a supper, Edith. I can hardly wait for dessert! In fact, I don't think I will. I have an errand to run."

"Please stay, Melissa. Things have gotten out of hand, I'm afraid."

"Yes, they have. Don't get up. I'll let myself out and phone you tomorrow morning, Edith."

When Edith and I resumed eating, I was sure that she would savage me for my treatment of her friend, but nothing of the kind happened. The best that she came up with after a silent stretch was, "You were cruel, Robert, but you may be right after all. The story I was going to tell you, Mrs. Agilesto's story, indicates that something funny's going on with Melissa. Didn't she just tell us that Agnes had left a couple days ago?"

"She was evasive, but Thursday's the impression she left with me," I replied, adding, "Mrs. Agilesto has quite a nose for local news, doesn't she?"

"You mean, she's a gossip? Yes. When Mrs. Agilesto came by this evening a little while before you came, she invited herself in. She said that there was something I really ought to know because she knew the two of us are friends. Mrs. Agilesto said that Melissa and Agnes had two huge fights. They happened recently. Apparently, it was all verbal. I can't imagine Melissa pulling hair. Anyway, Agnes is too big for her, I would think. Mrs. Agilesto said that Agnes shouted something about a swindle that Melissa had pulled and threatened to go to the police. After the second fight, Agnes and Melissa left the apartment together. Mrs. Agilesto thinks that they had made up their differences. I'm going to have a talk with Melissa to see if there is anything more to this."

"Do you think they really made up?" I asked. "It's hard to make up over a swindle, if that's the issue…"

"They could have been words said in anger. I'm surprised that the subject came up in the first place… swindling."

"You don't think that Melissa killed her so that she would not have to pay back wages?" I asked.

"This is no time for gallows humor, Robert."

"Rudy has too much money and is too taken with his work to adopt swindling. Right?"

"I should think so. He's honest enough to still pay the rent on this place."

That was news, and it disturbed me. So, I asked Edith if I had heard right.

"You did. I can almost pay for it now. Does my subsidy from Rudy bother you?"

"Is it alimony?"

"No. It's Rudy's generosity."

"What does Rudy get in return?" I asked.

"Well… my friendship. We agreed when we separated to remain close friends, and his subsidy is one of his ways of staying friendly. It's a gift. There's nothing wrong with that unless you think that every gift requires a counter gift. Do you believe in counter gifts, Robert?"

"Yes. Usually. They allow you to avoid outstanding obligations. I hate debts I can't pay quickly."

"Who says it's a debt? Do you consider supper here a debt that you have to repay?"

"No."

"The rent is a gift that Rudy can afford to give. What's more, he wants to give it. At first, I wanted to let him down gently. Now it's a way of staying in touch. We were man and wife."

"I was just curious. Does the check come from Rudy or Melissa?"

"Melissa. She handles a lot of Rudy's money, and it's a convenient way of handling the situation."

Given Edith's determination, I would either have to learn to accept her circumstances and her view of them or walk out. Being confused and needing time to think, I decided to stay, for a while anyway. Helping Edith to return the supper dishes to the kitchen, I speculated about Melissa, Rudy, and Agnes, and then asked Edith about a possibility that had been shaping up: "Could Melissa be cheating Rudy? I'd hate to see him in the right. Could that be the swindle that Agnes had mentioned?"

"I don't know. So much of this is speculation. Melissa has the opportunity because she advises him financially. Normally, I wouldn't think it of her. I suppose I owe it to Rudy to find out, or at least inquire."

Edith picked up her phone, dialed it, waited, and then set the receiver back on its cradle.

"No answer at Rudy's. I wonder where he is?" Edith mused.

"Melissa's?" I suggested.

Edith put off replying at first, but then we got to talking. Neither of us favored going down to Melissa's, routing the old girl out, seeing if Rudy were there, and creating a scene with accusations of swindle. Too little evidence had become apparent to risk that and risk more anger from Edith. Instead, the two of us retired for the evening. In the silence of a moment, I made a guarded pass at Edith, but she put me off gently, saying that she wasn't in the mood. My best avenue for self-expression denied, I opted for the second-best: sailing, or at least going to *Jupiter* for the night, getting a good rest, and starting out early the next morning, before the East Coast weather front forecast by the weather folks came through. Edith hesitated. Ever since Melissa had left in a huff, Edith had been pensive. With Rudy not answering his phone, she became more so.

"Why don't you go to *Jupiter* without me, Robert? I'll join you later."

"You want to go over to Rudy's, don't you?"

"Yes."

"And you don't want any company. No protection, right? Why don't I drive you there and wait outside for you?"

"I just don't want you along. I don't trust you with him. I know Rudy. You don't. I'll be safe as long as you are understanding, Robert."

"You'll be down to *Jupiter* later tonight?"

"Uh… don't wait up for me. I may not get there until tomorrow. I'll be safe. Don't worry."

What could I do? I could caveman it and endure extended passion and aggression from Edith. A caveman would pick her up on his shoulder and carry her away to some dank cave. Doing so raised my expectations that she would take off for the tall grass the first time I turned my back. The problem was, Edith had the strength and resilience of a hickory stick, and my arguing further with her would only have made her bitchy and determined to have her way; and my going to Rudy's house would only have compounded her aggravation and mine.

CHAPTER 12

Wrath of a Squall

Once on *Jupiter*, I paused in the chill of the night to scan the heavens. The moon hung on the decline. Sharing the firmament with it were several high, flat, thin clouds that looked like ghostly sand bars, shoals in a sea otherwise too deep to plumb. No sign of the planet *Jupiter*. Oddly enough, the sprays of stars up there, far from giving the illusion of bottom, furthered the impression of endless depths, accenting with their pinpricks of light the amount of darkness in which they were set. The firmament appeared devoid of life. Nevertheless, given the death of harvest and the desolation of late autumn at midnight, the earth at that moment seemed kin to its setting in the universe.

I slept late. The sleeping bag warmed me; the cabin did not. I broke through a minor web of fatigue and got up. After a breakfast of canned peaches, chilled from the cool of the night, I calculated the distractions that *Jupiter* could offer me.

These were the distractions of good works: cleaning the decks. Waxing the decks. Preparing the engine part way for winter by changing its oil and its filters, which meant starting and running the engine. Distractions of good works also meant more anti-winter work: pouring anti-freeze into every appropriate orifice on *Jupiter* and locating her winter cover in the boat yard's storage shed. I'd add anti-freeze to the engine itself after Edith and I returned from our sail. Such distractions offered virtue, some self-flagellation, and some redemptive movement. Under the warmth of the sun and the unseasonably warm weather that developed, my virtue faltered once again, and I picked up a book that I had been meaning to read for some time on how to forecast the weather. Such reading should enhance my chances at surviving the sea and at improving my mind. But, reading came hard because I kept thinking of Edith. I did not know if I was exercising the patience of a fool towards her or the forbearance of a saint. My hope was that, having lived with Rudy, she would still know how to handle him. Even so, would Rudy helplessly let her walk out of his life again to live with me, or would he let pride and anger override his affections and damn the consequence?

I thought of phoning Edith on the chance that she might have used an old-fashioned way to pacify him and had spent the night when doing so. Did I mind? Damn right, I did. My phoning would only aggravate the tension between the two of us. I didn't want to hector Edith back to Rudy, and I didn't want to provoke him by reminding him of his exile—such as it was— through divorce from Edith. All my figurings seemed futile because they depended on so little information. In the end, I could do little but stay where I was, trying to have faith that Edith would remain safe, and find still more distractions aboard *Jupiter*.

Warm and humid, the weather suggested the start of September rather than near the edge of November. A halo embraced the sun. The rest of the sky took on a red and whitish cast, a sign of moisture present in advance of a storm. The weather forecast on NOAA radio weather, on behalf of the gamblers in its audience, called for a thirty percent chance of showers—that's all. To get a broad view of the sky, I climbed on top of the coach roof and looked west: a high cloud ceiling was drifting in from that direction and was beginning to obscure the sun, but no mountainous thunderheads had appeared. No squall lines, the cavalry of the skies, and no war clouds either were in sight. No wind blew. Gray and silent, the sky rested in peace.

I was in the main cabin by the galley, on my hands and knees, looking through a shelf under the sink for a can of chicken noodle soup for lunch, when a car door slammed a few yards away in the parking lot. A woman laughed, Edith's laugh. I climbed out of the cabin onto the cockpit to see if I was right. I was. I did not believe who I saw with Edith: Melissa and Rudy. The three of them were carrying on without care, pain, or suspicion, if appearances could be believed. Except for Rudy and his bandages, they could have been the leads in a television soft drink commercial for the mature. A carefree pose of the mature. As they walked toward *Jupiter*, I wondered if they were conspiring to take me on the longest voyage of all. I was trapped in a bad dream.

"Permission to come aboard, Captain?" Edith asked.

I don't know where Edith picked up that bit of formality, but as a dig, it worked. It snapped me out of the spell I was in. The course of what Edith and I would say to each other was clear, though I kept it to myself: Why the company? I would ask. Her answer, in so many words, would be that she hoped to sort out what was troubling everyone by getting them together on a small yacht in a quiet cove, with good food, and away from disagreeable influences. After all, we should all be good friends, or that is what Edith thought, or so I calculated about this weird situation. I waited for someone, Edith most likely, to start the path to reconciliation and harmony. While I admired Edith's drive for diplomacy, I marveled at her lapse in taste and good sense. Also, what should I make of my own war between my tolerance and my good sense? As best I could, a legacy of my former life as a husband, I planned to go along with her lapse.

"Permission granted," I replied.

When Melissa, Edith, and, finally, Rudy climbed on board, they became quiet, probably tamed by my reserve. Rudy and Melissa each wore shoes with leather soles. Again, leather meant scuff marks for *Jupiter* that would have to be cleaned. Old as *Jupiter* was, I still did what I could to keep her blemishes to a minimum. Edith asked, "What's happening, Robert? Cheer up. I'll bet you want to know why there are four of us when two had been in order?"

"You're after peace, understanding, and harmony."

"Yes, Robert. There's nothing like a Sunday outing on a pretty day to clear up troubles. We're here to hold a council of peace and to go sailing. Is that all right with you? I would have called, but where can you find a land phone in the wilderness?"

I saw no way of telling her that she was trying to make past affections triumph over present realities. So now, my boat carried an expedition of forced friendship. The passenger list included one physician whose reverence for life had moved him to try and injure me, and maybe even kill me, and a young, old lady with murder in her eye and maybe poison from her food. This is what my true love brought to me. It didn't take long to reconsider my desire for settling down, for considering tolerance in the name of cohabitation and even marriage. Was I, after all, a kind and tolerant fool? I could tell them all to go to hell or at least to leave. Or I could play the rest of this handout for the adventure of it all. Adventure and my taste for black comedy won out. That, and my instinct for trying to make everything right and return to the harmony of Edith and I when we had spent time together since we met.

We resolved to sail to the Rhode River, where Edith and I had anchored on the first night at the start of when we were getting to know each other. Now, according to the plans of the day, the four of us would anchor, eat lunch, and talk. Melissa carried a large wicker basket that contained the meal. She had made deviled eggs and whatnots. Edith was responsible for the sandwiches, grapes, and wine. We ended up motoring, what with the air being still.

At anchor and while eating and listening to the desultory conversation, I checked the sky now and then. A darkening up north was the only change. The mood of the group after we had left Rudd Yard went from expectant to somber and silent, and even bored, given the lack of action. After lunch, however, I decided to force a little action and said:

"Since we're at a council of peace, we should know each other better. We'll have to get rid of our misunderstandings. Each of us will have to tell secrets."

Trying to rescue the situation from being gored by the silence that followed my statement, Edith asked me, "What are your secrets? You have a good many, it seems to me."

"It's not the secrets I know that keep all of us apart. It's the big one I don't know," I said, turning to Rudy, who all the while had become ever glummer. There was not much hope for truth from him, but so long as I was in this mess, the long shot was worth taking.

"Rudy, why did you put Earl Johnston up to attacking me on this boat?"

Everyone took a deep breath.

"I did no such thing," Rudy replied. "He was a patient of

mine. It's also true that some of the therapy I used on him, as I've explained to the police, may have aggravated his condition, though, in my experience, such therapy has worked to relieve tensions, not to increase them. It is also true," Rudy continued with a glance at Edith, "that I had cause to attack you. Nevertheless, as I've said before, the incidents with the car and the fence on your boat are as far as it ever went. I did not put my patient Earl Johnston up to assaulting you. His personality was such that any assault on you would have risked an assault on Edith. She's frustrating, but not that frustrating."

Edith laughed.

"How can I believe you?" I asked.

"The police seem to believe me. They let me go. Of course, they might arrest me again if you press your charges. Look, Robert, it's a tribute to your patience with me and your feelings for Edith that you're accommodating us with this sail."

Rudy looked tense as he said this. He continued, "To be frank with you, I can't cut Edith from my life. Remaining friends with her means staying on good terms with you."

"What do we have in common, except for Edith?" I asked, while silently trying to adjust to the twist in his argument. Another truly weird moment.

"Have a heart, Robert," Edith interjected. "Rudy wants accommodation. What's wrong with that? Are you that unsure of me? Our relationship," she said to me, glancing at Rudy, "stands on its own. How we get along with each other's friends does have a bearing on it."

Melissa remained quiet and watchful through all of this. At the risk of being a killjoy, I asked her, "How'd your session with the police go?"

Rudy perked up at this question.

"I haven't seen them yet, Robert. Surely, you're not going to start in with me again, now that you've tried and failed to cut Rudy down? Are you exercising your prerogatives as captain of this vessel? Holding us hostage, are you?"

Rudy cut in, "Melissa, he has reason enough to be critical of me. What's this about the police wanting to talk to you? About what?"

"I don't honestly know. If I did, I would have told you. I believe it may have something to do with the Earl Johnston affair, but I can't imagine what I could tell them that they don't already know."

"They're probably interested in your friendship with Earl Johnston," I contributed.

"It was hardly a friendship, Robert." Melissa smiled before continuing, "Edith said that this was to be a peace conference, Robert. When will we have peace and accommodation?"

"Melissa," Rudy said, "I didn't know that you were seeing one of my patients apart from our visits. Was it social?"

"I didn't think of Earl as just a patient, Rudy. He seemed in trouble, and I had supper with him once or twice just to cheer him up."

"He just didn't seem your type, or from your class," Rudy observed coolly.

The lapse in the conversation gave me a chance to go below and check the weather report on the radio. 163.55 on the marine radio dial brought in the same message: partly cloudy with a thirty percent chance of thundershowers. While the talk had been going on topsides, I'd noticed clouds darkening to the south and southwest, and they moved in haste. At first, I discounted that sign. But, even so, I began to figure on starting back to the yard because I did not want to get caught in a storm with a party of inexperienced sailors aboard. I started the engine and, while it was idling, went forward to haul in the anchor, refusing Rudy's offer of assistance.

Jupiter made the mouth of the Rhode River and was starting into the West River when the temperature gauge indicated that the motor was beginning to overheat. The motor sometimes did that when *Jupiter* had grounded and its propeller stirred muck from the bottom, muck that clogged the engine's water intake when under power. Other times, the motor heated up when the suction from the intake would capture a crab or a piece of debris. When that happened, the debris blocked the water intake to the engine, preventing the waters of the Bay from pumping through the engine and keeping her cool. The water intake blocked, I had to crawl into the tight engine compartment to unblock it. It would only take a minute or so to free up the intake, when I blew into the water intake hose after disconnecting it from the engine, before reconnecting it.

I turned off the engine and had Edith take the tiller and steer straight ahead while I ducked into the main cabin to work on the intake. Of course, bad luck could produce a gummed-up water pump. I could not tell. No time to tell. Fifteen minutes later, I emerged from the engine compartment, back into the main, darkened cabin. The trio outside in the cockpit sat up nervous and quiet.

"Is everything all right, Robert?" Edith asked. "The sky looks threatening."

A great darkness eclipsed the light from the southwestern half of the sky and moved rapidly to cover the gray light of the southeast. As I looked up, the scene suggested that all of us sat under the roof of a cavernous mouth that was about to close on us. I'd never seen a storm develop as quickly as this one. Only at the last moments of calm did I begin to see the low, speeding clouds of a line squall. A chill descended on us. The wind began to pick up. I told everyone to get into the cabin while I restarted the engine and took the tiller from Edith. She had gotten into the cabin and was helping Melissa down the short, steep stairs when the first assault arrived. It was as if a wall of wind struck us.

God knows what would have happened if the sails had been up. For once, my laziness worked for me. I had not wanted a repeat session of *Jupiter*'s going nowhere under slatting sails. As it was, the first wind of the storm assaulted *Jupiter* broadside, cuffing her almost onto her beam ends. I grabbed a lifeline stanchion next to me and had to let the tiller go for a moment. *Jupiter* veered under the onslaught, just short of capsizing, so it seemed. I thought the Bay would start climbing into the cockpit, and the boat would sink. Someone screamed from the cabin.

The only thing I could see was Rudy clutching the side of the main hatch and then falling into the main cabin, the boat still at an extreme heel from the force of the wind. More screams came from the cabin.

I managed to brace myself and lash the tiller during the wild confusion. The wind itself screamed through the rigging. Spray streaked past the boat, spray picked up from the river, and the spray and wind made it hard to see more than a few feet.

I had to do something quick because we had only a few hundred yards before we would run out of sea room and ground on the shoals where the West River runs into the Chesapeake. Someone was hurt in the cabin.

My first job was to stabilize *Jupiter*. That meant dropping the anchor and praying that it would hold. I clawed and scrambled my way to the bow. I had no time to put on a harness or life preserver. If I slipped, that could be it. No more troubles. Rain flooded down by the time I got to the anchor and wrestled it overboard and played out the rode. I could not see more than a few feet because of the storm. Despite the distractions of the storm, I let out the full length of the anchor rode.

Just before it went taut, *Jupiter* grounded lightly, enough to let me know we were in for more trouble. I hesitated to start the engine. Had I really cleared its intake? Would the engine overheat again? If it did overheat, we would be worse off than ever. Further, the wind blew far too strong for the motor to keep *Jupiter*'s bow into the wind, which meant that in any case the motor would have been useless.

I tried to haul in the anchor to keep *Jupiter* from grounding more, but the deck was pitching too much for me to get a secure footing, and the wind was pushing against the boat too hard. The grounding stopped for a while as *Jupiter* headed off to the south. Like most sailboats at anchor, *Jupiter* would pace first one way and then the other as the wind pushed against one side of the hull as if it were a sail, and then against the other, when *Jupiter* reached the end of her swing. In this instance, one end of her swing took her to water deep enough to carry her, and the other swing of the hull to shoals. The shoals, fortunately, were just deep enough to allow *Jupiter* to pound irregularly for a couple minutes at a time against them instead of getting stuck and worked over by the waves. *Jupiter* proved able to keep up her pacing. My boat's fate stabilized for the moment. So long as the anchor held, she would probably remain stable, barring the mast falling or the pounding causing the fiberglass hull to crack or break.

Hanging on as best I could, I made my way aft to the cockpit and into the main cabin. I shut the sliding cover of the main hatch to keep down the amount of rain and spray coming in.

Edith sat on the floor of the cabin, her legs braced against where the side of the dinette bunks met the floor or sole. She pushed her back against the front side of the galley. She had her right arm around Melissa's neck and shoulders; Melissa, apparently unconscious, her dress hiked up to her hips, sprawled on the part of the sole that extended into the forward cabin. On Edith's left lay Rudy, also on the floor, in a fetal position. Edith also held him in place, her left arm around the upper part of his body. The noise from the storm was so loud that I could hardly hear her say that Melissa had been badly injured. For her part, Edith seemed calm. There being little that I could do for them then, I returned my attentions to the cockpit to look after the fate of *Jupiter*.

The squall began to let up, even though the clouds remained. No sun, no rainbow. No time to relax, however, because there could always be another Chesapeake weather special along shortly. I wondered who might have died on the Bay. In fact, I found out later that, in the lower Chesapeake Bay, near Norfolk, Virginia, several people had lost their lives when the storm overwhelmed their large fishing boat, so fierce had the weather become.

As the weather and waters continued to grow calm I returned to the cabin. I checked the weather radio one last time and learned that, finally, it forecast severe storm warnings. Though the cabin was all wet, *Jupiter* had not taken enough water to put her in any danger of sinking. Luck had run out, however, so far as Melissa was concerned. Edith said that Melissa had probably broken a leg when thrown against the galley when the storm first struck. Melissa had fainted but would probably be reviving shortly. The terror of the storm had put Rudy into shock. He lay resting, apparently asleep on the floor. No point in stirring him up.

I hauled the anchor as the wind and the squall slacked; I got *Jupiter* underway while Edith remained below with the others, ready to comfort the injured. The motor worked fine. Go figure. After we made it to the Rudd Yard, Rudy had come to enough to examine Melissa. At the yard, he found a telephone and, not wanting to take chances even though Melissa showed spunk in recovery, phoned for an ambulance to take Melissa to a hospital. Edith took Rudy and herself to the hospital to be with Melissa. I phoned my insurance broker, telling him my version of the storm events and of the injury to Melissa.

CHAPTER 13

End of the Line

While walking to the car with Rudy, Edith called out over her shoulder that I would be on my own for a couple of days. Okay? Sorry about our getaway. She would, however, phone me. The way she had mothered Rudy during and after the storm, and her understandable skittishness toward me for the past few days, I figured I'd be lucky to get just a phone call. I also figured that some time apart from her could likewise be good for me, if only to reconsider how much patience it took to make me out as a true fool.

I stood there next to *Jupiter*, calculating how much I was up to enthusing myself into getting into the social hustings of the truly single again. The high drama of the afternoon had left me unenthused about my cooking supper. Annapolis, however, as mother of my fate at that moment, could offer a restaurant with a cheap meal. As long as I was in Annapolis, I might just as well talk to Detective Saugers in person, the better to read whether he was telling me all he could. Before I gave any thought about trying out a bar for the evening, reluctantly seeking, say, a "body exchange" where instant company, however bad, might be available, I phoned Saugers to see if he were at work and, if so, might be on the withered side of the Sunday shift for the Maryland State Police. I wanted to see if he had anything new about the Johnston killing and what he had to say about Melissa. He proved to be too busy to talk on the phone then. I would, however, be welcome to drop by his office. Be best if I phoned back in half an hour to make sure he would be free. Turns out, he was free and wanted to take a break from paperwork.

No problem walking through the police reception room, distinguished by a counter crowned by a bullet-proof introduction panel and desk complete with its sentry-receptionist. I walked further back along gray walls into a side-room, which featured Saugers' enlarged cubicle. Another moment went toward reflecting on Detective Saugers, especially his open manner toward me. He lacked the formal and sober caution of most police. He possessed fewer apparent defenses, as such, against a tricky world.

He looked up when I walked in, before smiling at me and saying, "You were right, Chappell. Johnston's place is spooky. Those handles in that big shower, they're something. Good for butchering deer and other game. We didn't find any bodies."

I responded to Saugers. "To bring you up to date, Melissa, Lady Melissa... the delusions of an aristocrat... the lady I told you about yesterday... She visited me this morning with a couple friends. She said she hadn't talked to you or any other police yet."

Detective Saugers replied, "She's a no-show. I drove over to her apartment this morning. I phoned her yesterday. We'd made an appointment. She stood me up. Maybe time for a warrant."

I told Saugers that Melissa had gone to the hospital, which he phoned for a brief conversation with a nurse. Melissa had left her room, maybe for a wheelchair stroll. His persuasiveness as a policeman enabled him to learn that Melissa had sprained her ankle but had broken nothing. Even so, the conversation continued; Melissa was due back from her walk. The nurse reassured Saugers that she would tell Melissa to phone him as soon as she returned.

It was quiet in the police station, the quiet of Sunday evening, when families should be ending a day of worship, rest, and relaxation according to the old school way of doing things. Saugers leaned back in his chair and sighed. Saugers divulged having talked with Melissa's hospital-assigned physician. "Chappell," he said, "I'll tell you a couple of things that Detective Byrne and I have discussed. We think, as the Johnston case stands, that you don't have to worry about protection... I mean, as far as your connection with Johnston is concerned, though you are not popular with some of the people at Knapp's Narrows. You achieved a poor reputation partly because of your relations with a young waitress, I believe."

"You talked with the manager of the Half Way House?"

"As you should know, we don't reveal or discuss who we talked to in our investigations."

"Betsy, the waitress, was young. She did know her way around. She's an adult in her knowledge of the world and how to make her way in it."

"No problem. But you might have cut it close with her."

"Okay. Fair point. I got caught in the lure of the moment. Why did you drop me as a suspect?"

"Your alibi checked out. We knew early on that you didn't know him and didn't have any obvious reason for killing him. Also, you have a clean record. There are a lot of others who did have reason to harm Johnston, so we have been spending our time checking them out. I can't say anything more about that, either. While you cut corners, you're not a criminal type. At least you don't fit any criminal profile."

"You think that Melissa and Dr. Alexander killed Johnston and tried to kill Edith?"

"I cannot tell you anything more, Chappell, at least for now."

After leaving Detective Saugers, I thought about Melissa, particularly the possibility that she might sue me. Her lesser injury might still give her, given how vindictive she was, reason enough to sue me. Why not pay her a visit and maybe save myself some trouble down the road?

The hospital proved to be almost as quiet as the barracks had been. When I asked at the admittance desk about Melissa, I learned that she was registered in room H1214; when I went there, the only trace of her presence was a mussed-up bed with no one in it. One of the nurses on duty said that Melissa had still not returned from her walk. On second thought, the nurse said, Melissa could not have gone far because of the severity of her sprain. A few minutes later, a plea went out over the hospital intercom for Melissa Kilmur to please return to her room. After a while more, a general alert went out over the hospital intercom about a missing patient. Melissa had disappeared into the night. She had left without paying her bill, or arranging to do so.

Detective Saugers was out when I phoned, so I left a message that Melissa had disappeared. I also phoned Edith and, when I couldn't raise her, tried Rudy, who likewise did not answer his phone. I figured that Edith probably would not have had time to return to her condo, assuming that she was on her way there. I made several more attempts to contact Edith and Rudy and even, on one occasion, Melissa, but failed to connect every time.

Finally, I phoned boss DeVon at her home and told her I'd be in to work the next morning.

"Don't be too sure, Chappell," she said. "My husband got a phone call when I was on the way home from the paper. He thinks that someone wants to get in touch with you about the problems you had with Earl Johnston."

"Do you or he know who called?"

"No. He didn't leave a name. He said he'd call back. My husband was rushed when he took the call, and didn't get much of an idea of what the caller was like except that he was young and had a country drawl. Where will you be?"

"I'm not sure."

"Well, check with me later this evening. I gather that you are still figuring out the story and the danger you are in."

"Yes. I'll check with you. Thanks for the latitude."

"There's not much room for latitude in this business, Chappell. Let me know when you have something to file. Call me at home if necessary. It's an unusual story."

After a quick supper at a fast-food restaurant, I planned to spend the night on *Jupiter* to avoid the drive to my room in Pasadena and back to Annapolis when I returned to work the next morning. I had turned on the lights of the main cabin and had unrolled my sleeping bag and sheets when *Jupiter* rocked slightly as someone came aboard. My first thought was that Detective Byrne had dropped by for another talk.

"Mr. Chappell," a man said. It was Red from the gas station where Earl's body had been found.

"It's late to go calling, Red," I answered. "You're a long way from Knapp's Narrows. What are you doing here, anyway?"

"I want to talk to you about something."

"How'd you find me?"

"Betsy told us where you work. Your boss said where you'd most likely be."

"Is Betsy okay?" I asked.

"She's gone. Nothing for you to concern yourself with."

Red and two studs in their early twenties climbed down into the cabin. He said, "Mr. Chappell, I'd like you to meet Betsy's boyfriend, Mike."

Mike was as tall as I was and had a smooth air about him, as if he were a seal from an aquatic park. He also looked unhappy, as if straining at his gut.

"You all out for revenge?" I asked.

"Could be," Red replied. "What did you tell the cops about us? They're looking for us. I want to know what to tell them."

"I'll tell you when we get off the boat. It's too cramped in here."

Instead of waiting for us to get off *Jupiter*, they made a grab for me in the cabin. Not much room for them and me to maneuver. I tried to get to the main light switch to turn off the lights and start a quick round of hide and seek. A hit on my head, however, stopped me short.

When I came to, everything was dark. My hands were tied behind me, and I lay on the forward part of the cargo bay of a van.

There was no pleasure in the pain in my head. The van sped along a deserted country highway, dark except for an occasional light that we passed. Mike sat away from me, his back resting against the rear doors of the van. To escape, I would have to go through or around Mike. Something pressed against my butt, another discomfort. The boys in their haste had overlooked my pocketknife—I was in the company of amateurs. The knife offered hope, but I did not want to make a move until my head cleared.

I tried to sort out what was happening. Red and the gang must have been in a lot of trouble to chance a kidnapping charge, if they had thought at all about such trouble or risk. Since they hadn't come just for money, or so it seemed, they probably sought information about the Johnston family and their money, particularly what I had learned from my investigation of them. They were probably also after revenge because of Betsy, especially considering Red's initial reaction. They had, after all, taken out after me at Knapp's Narrows in a boat. Now, the presence of Mike. I remembered suggesting to Red that I had watched him and his friends burn down the Johnston place. That inspiration of the moment, in retrospect, was probably unwise.

I shifted my position to make it easier to get at my pocketknife. Mike saw me move and said to Red and the other fellow in the front seats, "Guess we didn't kill him after all, guys. We'll get some more sport out of him yet, the son of a bitch."

He moved next to me and untied the gag over my mouth, and said, "You make a wrong move or say the wrong thing, and

I'll cut you into little pieces. Then you won't make any wrong move or say the wrong thing. Understand?"

"Yes."

"What did you tell the cops?"

I could tell Mike and the others the truth and wait for them to sport with me in cold blood. Or I could lie and, though my fate would probably be the same, I would have the pleasure of knowing that they were sweating, not knowing for sure what I'd divulged to the cops. So, I lied: "I told them about how you all torched the Johnston place. The cops are supposed to have me under surveillance."

"Yea," Mike said, "they're real cool about it. You're a victim of cop delay. We watched your boat for an hour, and nobody's made their move. Red, can you see any cops?"

Red and the other fellow laughed with a trace of nasty cheer.

"Looks like you've got a tough break, Mr. Chappell," Mike said.

"Maybe. But you're in for trouble too. As it is, you've got a kidnapping charge added to the other offenses."

"The cops can't prove nothing after we get through with you."

"Who else are the cops going to look for when I turn up missing? You're going to be running away from here for the rest of your life. That or doing time. The cops want you because they figure anyone who'd burn down the Johnston house was a suspect in Earl's death. They're just waiting to make their move, and you know it. That's why you came for me."

"No shit!" Mike replied. "Tell me about it."

"We're doing the figuring, asshole," Red contributed from the front.

We had been traveling on a main road for some time. At one point, I saw a row of stores like ones on the road to Ocean City. Those stores meant the boys had taken me across the Bay Bridge to the Eastern Shore, to Earl's country. We probably would get off the good road at some point so that they could have their sport; maybe go to some secluded place where they wouldn't be disturbed in their revels with me. Earl's place in the deep woods would be perfect. I wondered if the police had a watch on it. Probably not. A watch would take more people on the force than they had. If it were Earl's place, my best chance would be to find some way to free myself and some way to escape to the woods around it, for woods, despite the lack of mercy its creatures normally showed to one another, might hide me. All this required luck which then seemed in short supply.

"Hey, asshole," Red called out. "What did Betsy tell you about us?"

"What do you mean?"

"Mike!" Red ordered, "Give him a kick. If he don't give us straight answers fast, we'll start to operate on him in the van like we did on Earl."

"You hear him?" Mike asked.

"Yep. Betsy didn't say anything to me, Red. You're the one who told me how unpopular the Johnstons were and how they were going to leave one way or another. I just put two and two together."

"That's funny," Mike said. "While I was beating the hell out of her for spending the night with you, she said she'd told you everything."

Someone had dealt me a joker.

I replied, "An angry woman will say anything. She didn't like me. She didn't like you. So, she went to the cops herself to stick it to you, and she dumped the blame for whatever she told the cops on me for my reward."

Mike kept quiet. He had returned to his former post and, dozing now and then, leaned against the back doors of the van while it drove on. Little by little, I fished the knife out of my pocket. I almost dropped the blade as I struggled to open it, my movements hampered by the clothesline the boys had used to bind my wrists. The clothesline cut easily. I had to make my move before long.

My chance came to talk to Red directly when I faced toward the open windows enough to see forward but not so much as to show Mike I'd cut the bonds on my hands. Lights from a large farm came into view, and beyond them, I could see woods. Just before a country road turned off toward the farm, there stood a gas station, still open for business.

I moved quickly but not in panic. I placed my left arm around Red's neck and put my right hand with the open knife blade in it just in front of Red's right eye.

"I can't see!" Red shouted while he stomped on the brakes. The van skidded to a stop, ending up partly in a ditch by the side of the road.

"What the fuck!?" Red screamed.

"Keep cool, or I'll stab him in the eyes and carve his brains out. Nobody move!" I screamed.

"Get away!" Red shouted at his sidekicks, and they moved toward me to try and disarm me. "Don't touch him, Mike! John!"

We were at a standoff for the moment.

"Get out of the van!" I directed Mike and John, shouting at them so they would have no doubts about what I might do. "Stand in front of the van, where I can see you."

They hesitated.

"Do what he says," Red ordered.

Mike and John got out of the van and stood in the headlights as ordered.

"What are you going to do now?" Red asked.

"Wait. That's all, unless you or the others try something funny." The blade of my knife stood a half an inch or so from Red's right eye. My right arm lay braced on Red's right shoulder. I continued to stand in a crouch, half behind, half above Red, making sure the blade stayed where it should. My left arm continued its chokehold around his neck. In one of the mirrors of the van, I could see the lights from the road to the farm we'd passed, no more than fifty yards back, maybe a hundred. Lights from the gas station showed just ahead of us. I hoped that the folks at the gas station or farm would see the truck and come to see if everything was all right.

"You're making me nervous," Red said.

"Right!" I replied.

Time passed slowly. My cramped position made me tired, but I had no choice but to hold it. So that Red did not get any false hopes about making a quick move and freeing himself, I told him to relax and lightly rested the blade of my knife on his cheek, just below his eye. I told him he could not afford to move or even to think about moving.

A little while later, Red began to talk in a soft voice, saying that he and his friends only wanted to ask me a few questions and scare me good because I had fooled around with Betsy. It was only natural, he continued, for them to want to know what I had told the cops. As for their talk about what they had done to Earl, that was only fooling, something to scare me with. They hadn't really done anything to Earl. Yes, I replied, that was clear from the police photos of the body. It must have been the wrong body, Red responded. I told Red to keep quiet and keep on relaxing.

The wait paid off eventually when a state trooper pulled up in his patrol car next to us. He rolled down his window and said, "I got a report from the gas station that you are a suspicious presence. You all are not out looking for trouble. Thinking of robbing the gas station? What about spotlighting deer? You have a buck or a doe in the back of the van?"

"No, officer, these hotshots are trying to kidnap me."

The trooper called for assistance over his radio. He got out of his car, gun drawn, and ordered Red and me out of the truck and then told the four of us to lean against the truck and spread our legs. Mike and John, however, continued to stand in the glare of the car and truck lights.

"You two in front of the truck. Don't you hear me?"

"We was only out having a good time, officer," Red said as Mike and John began to walk past the cop. Without warning, Mike and John, as they passed the trooper, tried to jump him. The cop fired his gun at John, who doubled up and fell, as Mike seemed to punch the cop in the belly. The cop fell too. As Mike pulled his arm back, I could see that he held a long switchblade knife and that he had stabbed the cop with it. John lay on the ground, screaming and writhing while the trooper lay nearby, quiet as a stone. Red ran over to the cop and grabbed the gun from his hand, while I ran for my life.

I scrambled around the back end of the van, into darkness and underbrush by the side of the road and headed toward the woods. The crack of a gunshot sounded, and a bullet grazed my head. Running from light to dark blinded me. I stumbled in a ditch but caught myself and kept on running.

"Where the fuck is he!?" Red called out.

"Over there, Red!" Mike replied. "I can hear him."

I reached a stand of tall brush. Though my eyes were becoming adjusted to the dark, I still couldn't see much, so I had to feel my way quietly. The wound on my head throbbed. Despite my slow progress, I put some distance between myself and my pursuers, whom I could hear crashing about in the brush near the road. Where were the cops? It was time to take a breather.

A short time later, the beam of a flashlight lit up part of the woods near me. I thought about running further in the woods in the hope that I would lose Red and Mike for good. But the flashlight revealed little cover in the deeper parts of the woods. The crown of the forest there grew too densely, too close together, to allow enough light to support much brush on the floor, next to the base of the trunks. It would be like trying to hide in a huge courtroom or even a cathedral, with nothing to serve as cover, except for a few large pillars. The forest offered majesty but little protection. My best bet was to stay in the thicket that I had found, lying prone at the base of a young, bushy evergreen.

The flashlight came closer. Red and Mike at one point asked each other if he saw anything. At one time, they could not have been any more than twenty feet away, their light flicking above me for a moment. Red decided that they had looked for me long enough and agreed to take off before more cops arrived. They would always have another chance at me.

One siren, then several of them, keened shortly after the flashlight disappeared. Trying to make it to the farm that we had passed seemed like a good idea to me. So was staying put until everything calmed down and I had a chance to think. But I opted instead for going to the road and trying to hitch up with the police. Lights flashing in quick time from the road guided me, for the way was dark, and in the confusion I had lost track of where the road lay.

Police cars were parked all over the road near the van, surrounded by at least fifteen Troopers. Their own man being down and not moving, the Troopers were ready to tear me apart when I approached them. I told the police who I was and what had happened and guessed that Red and Mike were still in the woods. The troopers organized search parties, one of which headed toward the farm just as shots rang out from that direction. I got into one of the police cars with the troopers, and we took off toward the shots.

In a minute or two, we arrived at the entrance of the road to the farmhouse and drove in. What should we see but a trio: a man in his late fifties, balding and paunchy, with blue jeans on the bottom and fitting into army boots, and pajamas as a top? He held a shotgun on Red and Mike, who were standing there in the barnyard, arms raised up toward a lone streetlight that illuminated the barnyard. As the troopers and I began to get out of the cars, the farmer asked us in a loud voice, "What the hell took you so long?"

CHAPTER 14

Not As Much Fun

I spent the rest of the night with the police, answering their questions without number. I wrote of my kidnapping, murder, and narrow escape before I woke up boss DeVon (patient though intermittently cranky while I dictated my account over the phone). Only then did I sleep late. Eventually, I made it into the *Herald* in the middle of the afternoon.

By the time I arrived, the *Herald* had published on page one the story of how the Maryland State Police had rescued me and arrested Red, Mike, and John (in critical condition) for the murders of Maryland State Trooper Stephen Greer and of Earl Johnston. Maryland police continued to investigate the murder and its consequences. The draw of my version of the story was, after all, an "I was there" exclusive that violated a classic journalistic doctrine that no reporter shall deliberately be the center of the news. To put the doctrine another way, news, with rare exceptions, shall always describe what happened to someone else. I then read through the *Baltimore Sun* version of my story.

I phoned Detective Saugers to find out if anything else had broken on the case. He was busy and starved for time. He asked that I call again before supper, which I did. Saugers was still busy, so he made it quick: "Chappell, John is still in the hospital, in critical condition with his gunshot wound. So, if he survives, we'll only have murder charges against Red and Mike."

"When will Trooper Greer be buried?" I asked.

"Not arranged yet. His wife is really broken up over it. We all are."

"Is there anything I can do to help? He saved my life."

"Not that I know of. We're still interested in your other friend, Melissa. You were right. She's skipped town. Incidentally, one of Earl Johnston's buddies has shed some light on your problem. He was drinking with Johnston a couple days before the assault on you. The buddy claims that Johnston bragged how he was going to earn big money for killing some broad and beating up on her boyfriend. Johnston apparently told his buddy that a rich lady friend of his shrink had suggested the attack."

"What was the motive?" I asked.

"Don't know. That's one of the things I wanted to talk to Mrs. Kilmur about. She's got a track record, mostly for fraud. Her late husband carried a couple charges of swindling too. She's a kind of black widow. Whoever she was helping, she was helping herself too. There's one other thing. We can't do much about your assault charge unless you want to press charges against Dr. Alexander. Do you want us to do so?"

"No. It looks as if Lady Melissa was behind most of the trouble anyway."

"Don't hold your breath for us to catch her, Mr. Chappell. She's a professional submarine, and she's learned to stay submerged in other places for long periods, I expect. She hired the best lawyers. How long did your friend, Edith, know her?"

"Several years, anyway."

"That's what I understand. Mrs. Kilmur apparently took off on so-called business trips now and then. So did her husband. I guess she's off on another one."

Finally, about two weeks later, Edith phoned me. I had given up trying to contact her because, after a call to her office, I learned that she too had left town on vacation. When Edith talked to me, she did so in haste, as if she did not want to spend any time on her out-of-town adventures. She asked that we sup that evening—Friday evening, in fact—in a romantic place, the Clam Pier in Galesville. A dark moment came over my judgment when I asked myself whether, in this age of the grotesque and unlikely, Edith and Rudy had taken off together.

What to think about Friday evening? It marked the entrance to Sunday, the start of a new week, with new possibilities for the future, maybe even life heading in a new direction. Slow as I was and patient beyond good sense, I was long overdue to see what Edith had in mind for our future, if any, and compare how the his and her of this matched.

The Pier restaurant offered its usual comfortable hospitality, even though the winter shrinkage of business there had begun. On schedule, the restaurant's porch was closed until April Fools' Day, in deference to winter and the hope of Spring. Though the Pier contained several other large rooms, the center of action for the duration remained the combined bar and small dining room—a den with plenty of wood on the walls and ceiling, and with a fireplace, all of it for the evening hibernation of the guests of the restaurant, closeted for the moment from the liberties of the great world outside. I sat, comforted by an old reliable, gin and tonic, and a clear view of the fire that warmed my bones.

Now and then, I parked my thoughts and looked beyond the great, round timbers that supported the ceiling and at the hewn beams that helped to frame the room. A look at the darkness out the window revealed several large, blackened spider webs in the corners of the windows. More agreeably, my view of the docks revealed once again numerous boats, ranked and filed in their slips, and in various fashions wrapped in canvas and otherwise prepared for winter. Most of the multitude of boats could only be dimly seen outside, a forest of aluminum spars silhouetted against a few, small, distant marina lights. Other smaller and fainter lights shown from houses and a yacht club on the far side of West River. On the river itself, no green or red or white boat lights moved up or downstream. Only a few lambent reflections on the water interrupted what otherwise appeared to be a void.

Edith arrived, an animated fashion plate, having gone all out for our supper. She wanted to make an impression and did. She was on her good behavior as if she had done something that she knew would cause trouble between us. I took a guess by asking, with a smile:

"How was your vacation with Rudy?"

"Who told you?" She caught herself and managed to smile back.

"Nobody. Just an easy guess."

"Have you guessed yet what happened to Melissa? You, Robert, were wrong about Rudy, but right about her. He's had an accountant go over his estate. Would you believe that Melissa borrowed—probably embezzled—a lot of money from him. So did her husband? She was into Rudy for more than $150,000."

"The police are after her. They have been for some time," I replied.

"Now, with what I know, I'm not surprised. Disappointed? Yes. Betrayed? Yes again. The Maryland police came by and asked me about her. So did two Washington, D.C., detectives. They're after her about a swindle she may have pulled against a stockbroker, of all people. That's talent. She also seems to have defrauded a close relative of Agnes' from Ohio—the relative has filed a complaint against Melissa. That's what Agnes meant by the swindle, I guess. I wonder what happened to her? The manager of my apartment building says that Melissa was way behind in her rent. He's after her too. How could she be short of money? It makes me sick to think that Melissa and I were so close. But I didn't know what she was up to… You know, Robert, I still think she had genuine affection for me. That's why, even when the police were closing in on her, she came sailing with us."

"That and wanting to see if there was any last-ditch out from her problems," I said. "So, when was the last time you heard from her?"

"Not since we put her into the ambulance. Do you think Melissa put Earl Johnston up to the assault on us?"

"Yes. She probably thought Rudy would be easier to devour if she could feast alone with him, with him grieving over your death."

Edith winced at that remark. Her reaction led me to consider why she had suggested supper. Had she tired again of Rudy? Did she want us to take up where we had left off, wherever that was? Or, did she want the two of us to go our separate ways? As it turned out, she favored a middle course, a course which she hesitantly suggested after I said that her vacation with Rudy indicated that I might be hearing their wedding bells soon.

"To tell you the truth, I'm in a fix, Robert. I feel responsible for Rudy. I may even marry him again. In my way, I love him. But… I don't know how to say this—and you'll probably laugh at me, or God knows what—but… I still care for you. I like to be around you… most of the time anyway, apart from our recent adventures on the water. We do get along well, probably because you do not fall into the trap of long-range plans. Such plans can be a prison. What I'm trying to say is that Rudy is my responsibility, and you are my vacation and my pleasure."

That was quite a line to swallow. I replied, "Are you after part-time domesticity? You want to hedge your bets?"

"You could say that. Your fling with the waitress tells me that you like a little independence mixed with a little domesticity. You know, Rudy and I are alike. Each of us needs fundamental diversions. He has his medicine. I have him and, well, you're free and unattached, and I'd like to keep on seeing you too."

"How does Rudy feel about this?"

"He'll accept it. He'll even continue to be pleasant to you, for my sake. Why are you hesitating, Robert? You're not getting tired of me, are you?"

"Not at all."

"Something's on your mind, Robert. You're not thinking of something more formal for us… such as marriage?"

"With you and Rudy tying the knot again? You mean a triple wedding? Would that be appropriate?"

"Robert! You're not going to confide in me? Little old me?" The original temptress, she smiled broadly.

"Well, to confide in you," I said, "I have wondered at one

time or another if we might tie the knot. But... Let's remain friends. Philosopher friends."

"You mean platonic?" she asked, laughing.

"Yes."

"It's not as much fun."

"Probably not. It has the advantage of keeping all—or at least most of—our cards on the table."

"So, you're after full ownership—whatever that is—over variety? Uh, except for a lapse now and then."

"Edith... I'm looking for settling down. Family life. Kids. Whatever family life should provide. My run at the single life is old hat."

"So, Robert, you think that you can find enough to keep you interested in the 'same old, same old?' You already tried family before your divorce. What changed your mind?"

"Aging—I'm not old yet, but it's coming. Aging works best with good company. That should begin with family. Family should mean good company that lasts as long as you feel the need for touch—sex and what comes with it. You're great company when you are available. With you, part-time harmony or good company works. That's not enough for me."

"Is this your way of saying goodbye? Fun while it lasted?" Edith asked.

"Well... yes... that's one way of putting it."

"So, you hope or plan to live a settled life as a reporter? Even though your life will always hang on what is coming next? The lure of the next surprise? The next adventure in the midst of the ordinary and the chaotic?"

"It looks that way. To each his or her own. Goodbye and good luck with Rudy, Sweetheart," I said.

"I'll miss you."

About the Author

For decades Jim Sayler has lived up to his last name by boating under sail and power on the Chesapeake Bay. Sailing offers him a way of life that has given him a break from duress when he worked as a writer, starting as a cub reporter for the *Washington Star*. Sayler's study of human nature continued as an analyst for Congress, employed by *Congressional Quarterly*. Then, he began a 30-year career on Capitol Hill with the Congressional Research Service of the Library of Congress, becoming a senior analyst and editor. Sayler took a break from Capitol Hill as a journalist-research writer for the *New York Times*; a trade book editor for *Reader's Digest's Funk and Wagnalls*; and then writing radio news for the Columbia Broadcasting System's NewsRadio 88 in New York City. Altogether, with a few lethal risks, a career of adventure. Jim Sayler. Rockville, Maryland.